a cherished petal

The downside of being roped into dying 100 eggs for the Petrie's Crossing Easter Egg Hunt? Well...dying 100 eggs without cracking any shells. But there's an upside that makes Shannon smile. Getting included in the town's celebrate-every-holiday obsession is a good sign she's been accepted.

After a month-long break from her Aunt Caroline's trinkets box, enjoying Mitch's cooking, Shannon takes the gloves off for a set of vintage hairpins. The moment her fingers touch aged gold and pearls, she envisions a frightened teenage woman running away with her unborn child's father. The mystery deepens with the discovery the young woman was reported missing and never found.

The problem is, Shannon's visions have revealed details that could close a cold case—but break a family's hearts. Can she return the trinkets while withholding the truth? Or will trusting one person too many cause a backlash that could drive her away from all she loves—her adopted home town, her friends, even Mitch?

Lost Trinket Series
a timed wager
a ring of truth
a secret escape
a hushed favor
a guarded decree
a sacred devotion
a cold hour

****

Heroes of Coweta County
Ghostdrums
Sweet Fatalities

****

Salem's Embrace

a cherished petal

Lost Trinkets Series Book Eight

Sherrie Lea Morgan

Village Publishing

ACWORTH, GEORGIA

Sherrie Lea Morgan/Village Publishing
PO Box 2519
Acworth, Georgia/USA 30102
www.sherrieleamorgan.com

This is a work of fiction. Names, places, characters and incidents are either the product of the author's imagination or are used fictitiously, and any resemblance to any actual persons, living or dead, organizations, events or locales is entirely coincidental.

Book Layout © 2017 BookDesignTemplates.com

a cherished petal/The Lost Trinkets Series Book Eight/Sherrie Lea Morgan. – 1st ed.
Editor: Lindsey Loucks
Cover for this book done by Yocla Designs
ISBN 978-1-949256-13-0

This book is dedicated to Kathy, who still won't share her potato salad recipe.

psychometry (sī kämətrē) noun

1. the ability to discover facts about an event or person by touching inanimate objects associated with them.

manifestation (manəfes tāSH(ə)n) noun
d: an occult phenomenon; specifically: *materialization*

Medium (mēdē əm)

1. A person claiming to be in contact with the spirits of the dead and to communicate between the dead and the living

psy·chic (/ ˈsīkik/) noun

1. A person considered or claiming to have psychic powers; a medium.

ghost (gōst) noun
1. The soul of a dead person believed to be an inhabitant of the unseen world or to appear to the living in bodily likeness.

Forensic Psychic
1. A person who investigates crimes by using purported paranormal psychic abilities.

Meditation
Meditation is the practice of turning one's attention to a single point of reference. It can involve focusing on the breath, bodily sensations, or on a word or phrase, known as a mantra. In other words,

meditation means pivoting away from distracting thoughts and focusing on the present moment.

Vision
3.c. direct mystical awareness of the supernatural usually in visible form

contents

Chapter One

"One hundred eggs? Are you kidding me?"

Maggie grinned shaking her head. "Nope. Everyone provides dyed eggs for the big Easter Egg hunt."

I held up a hand, grinning, "Wait a minute. You really think you could fool me with that one? Come on, Maggie. You could have come up with something better than that." I shook my head. "You almost got me there." I chuckled.

Maggie tipped her head to the side quizzically. "What are you talking about?"

"A hundred decorated eggs? Really?"

"I'm serious," she said.

"It's April Fool's Day and I'm not falling for that."

Her mouth dropped open, then she closed it quickly before responding. "You think this is a joke?" She held out the flyer. "Here look at it."

I waved it away. "I could have done something up on the computer too."

"Shannon, I'm not joking. I'm sorry, but Bobby dropped off this flyer this morning."

I pursed my lips. She seemed serious and my stomach clenched. *Another town celebration? It can't be.* I tipped my head. "Did you get him on your side too?"

She shook her head. "No, I didn't. I swear. Besides, I hate April Fool's Day. I'd never try to pull something like this on you. I know how upset you get at being forced to participate in the town's celebrations."

"I only get upset because I'm never asked. The mayor just assumes we'll do it and acts like it's our duty as business owners."

She lifted then dropped a shoulder, "It is our duty. If we didn't participate, who would?"

"But so many? I mean, practically one per month is a lot."

"Keeps up the morale of the town."

"You really believe that?"

She nodded. "I do. In small towns like Petrie's, morale can drop too fast because of the economy. I think everyone is afraid of it turning into a ghost town and being forgotten like so many other small towns. The good thing is Petrie's was never dependent on a big corporation. It doesn't hurt with having a large university in Augusta, either. Still, people worry and the town council figures the celebrations help keep people involved and happy."

I planted my hands on my hips. "So, you're serious about the egg hunt? You're not pulling my leg?"

"I am very serious, and I promise I'm not joking."

"Where are we going to get a hundred eggs? How on earth are we going to get that many dyed?" Dratted small-town celebrations. I should have known it the first time they forced me to participate in a celebration. I'm stuck and I'm never getting out of this. "I'm closing Trinkets, so I don't have to do these things anymore."

"Oh, come on. It'll be fun. Andy's kids will help."

"Ricky works at the Museum, so he'll be stuck helping, or rather doing the dye jobs for her place." I winked. "Because we all know Judy wouldn't dare be caught with colored dye on her hands."

"No, he won't. Rocky's doesn't have to provide any eggs."

I jerked back. "Why the heck not?"

"The Mayor drew names and there are only three businesses dying eggs. We don't really need that many eggs."

"One hundred eggs? The entire population of Petrie's barely exceeds that."

"Cheer up, it'll be fun."

I scowled. "Fun? I bet the Mayor lied and said Trinkets without even pulling our name. He's still mad about the whole cemetery debacle."

15

Maggie laughed while handing me the flyer Bobby delivered earlier. I quickly scanned the words, shaking my head.

"I knew Bobby was up to no good when he said he was here to see you instead of me. He knew how ticked off I'd be."

She shrugged. "He's not stupid, he didn't want you to shoot the messenger."

I stared at her considering her words and behavior. I grinned. "You know what? You're right. We should be honored to be chosen to dye one hundred eggs for the event. In fact, now that you're a manager here, I'll leave the details up to you."

"Wait, what?" her jaw dropped.

"Yep. Congratulations on your promotion. Let me know when the eggs are ready to be dyed and I'll be here."

"No fair," Maggie crossed her arms across her chest. "Promote me so you don't have to organize the egg dying. That's low."

"Yep. I love owning a business." I busted out laughing so hard, I bent over to catch my breath.

"You're awful," she said with a smile.

"I know," I sucked in air. "I know." Ducking the light punch she aimed at my shoulder, I danced away, placing the sales counter between us for safety. "It'll be fun." Holding my hands up, I winked.

"You may be safe now, but wait. I'll get you back."

I shrugged. "Whatever. As long as I don't have to coordinate getting that many eggs over here, boiled, prepped for dying, do your worst."

She winced. "I forgot about boiling them." She held out her hand. "Let me see if the diner is going to do that for us or if we have to do it ourselves."

Handing over the paper, I leaned against the sales counter. "Hopefully you won't have to do that part too. What are the other businesses who aren't decorating eggs doing?"

"Helping out with decorating the park, donating for vendors."

"The kids are going to have a blast. I can't remember ever hunting for Easter eggs when I was little. Did you do it?"

Maggie glanced up from reading. "Of course. My parents, then Grandma would hide them. After church we'd go searching and fill our baskets while they prepped for lunch."

"You find a lot?"

"I found my fair share. My cousins used to try to steal them out of my basket, but I made up for the missing ones by getting the best seat at lunch."

"Which was?"

"Next to Grandma," she said waving the paper. "It says on the back of the flyer that the diner is going to hard boil them for us first."

"Thank goodness." *Poor Mitch.* "We got lucky there."

"Yep. You want to do simple colors or anything special?" Maggie asked.

"You're in charge, so whatever you want to do. Remember, if we have Andy, Nancy and Clara helping, we can't do anything too fancy."

Her eyes widened. "Know what? We could do those little shrink wrap decorations. That'd be less messy."

"Sounds good."

She folded and tucked the event notice into her pants pockets. "By the way, it's been almost a whole month and you haven't mentioned returning any other items. Are you done returning the items?"

"Nope. I was just taking a break. Not sure if I want to try to do one with this Easter thing going on."

"Why not? It's only dying eggs and I'm coordinating everything."

"True. Its just things tend to get messy when I return an item and I'm not sure I want to bring that possibility into the town right now."

"Petrie's Crossing celebrates nearly every major holiday on the calendar along with some odd ones too. It's not like you're going to find a whole two months without anything going on to return items."

"I suppose I could do another." Stretching my arms above my head, I let the image of my little box of trinkets flit into my mind. Immediately, a picture of the small hairpins appeared with their little pearl centered gold flowers. Well, I guess the item made the   decision.   *Great.*

Chapter Two

After closing for the day, I headed home stopping by the diner to say hi to Mitch. The bustling kitchen amazed me every time I stepped inside it, with everyone moving almost like in a well-choreographed dance between the stoves, oven and prep area. Sliding inside and staying close to the wall and out of the path of the cooks, I watched in awe. Mitch glanced over while stirring a large pot of sauce causing the aromas of basil, thyme, and tomatoes to lift and fill the air. My stomach grumbled reminding me, once again, I forgot to eat breakfast. Scratch that, I forgot lunch too. Shoot. I lifted a brow in his direction, and he chuckled, before stretching over the counter and grabbing a to-go box. He spooned in curled pasta, then ladled some of the bubbling sauce over it, tossed in a large piece of bread, closed it and brought it to me. My mouth watered as soon as I grabbed it out of his hands. He dropped a kiss on my cheek, whispered sweet nothings in my ear which made my body warm and face flush. Dang I loved this man. He winked, and then pointed toward the exit.

That was my cue to leave. All but skipping out the door, I headed home.

Once there, I aimed for the kitchen, tugged open the box and inhaled deeply to the bouquet of scents from the fresh cooked pasta. Grabbing utensils, along with a bottle of water, I sat and filled my belly, letting images of the last few weeks of my newfound domestic life flit around my mind. Providing a hundred eggs for the town's Easter Egg Hunt was a small price for this life I led. I'd dye two hundred. I blinked. No. Not two hundred. After scarfing down dinner, I cleaned up and made my way to my office. Once there, I took time to go through my routine of lighting incense, candles, setting out crystals and punching on the music for relaxation. Sitting behind my desk, I opened the drawer, took out and slipped on my gloves, then lifted the box of trinkets, setting it on my desk. Leaning back, I closed my lids and completed three rounds of my breathing exercise, calming my mind and body in preparation for a reading. Opening the box, I lifted out the hairpins and studied them. They looked as though they'd been used around the fifties or sixties in the intricate up dos of higher society women. Interesting. I slipped off my gloves, lifted and held the pins in the palms of my hands, then closed my lids again allowing my mind to open for a vision.

"We don't have a choice, babe," he said.

The young woman placed a hand across her slightly bulging belly. "But Brian, Mamma gave me those to pass on to the baby."

"If we don't sell them, we won't have the money to run away. Your parents want you to give our child up for adoption. You don't want that any more than I do," he said. "It's the only way we can afford to get out of this town and start a new life together." He stroked a finger down the young woman's cheek. "You and me babe, we can do this together. I promise."

She nodded and handed him the golden hairpins. "Do you think Mr. Green will tell on us?"

He shook his head. "I don't know. That's why you have to pawn them. He'll wonder if I do it."

"But if he asks, what should I say?" Her brows furrowed. "He might call Mamma and Daddy."

"Babe, he won't if you tell him it's to get the baby things you need," he paused, placing a hand over hers, which remained on her stomach. "If you convince him you're trying to be independent, he won't say anything."

"Will you come with me?" She asked.

He shook his head. "I can't. I'm going to get the car, you got your suitcase ready?"

She nodded.

"Then tonight, before your Daddy gets home from work, meet me out back with your bags. I'll toss them in the car and drive around to the back alley behind the pawnshop. Once you get the money from there, go around back and we'll leave."

"I'm scared," she whispered.

"I'm not. I'll be brave for both of us. Come on," he wrapped his arms around her. "Once we leave, we can go someplace away from here and start our lives. Don't you want that?"

"Yes," she said, then lifted her face to his. He kissed her. "And we'll get married once we're out of here?"

He nodded. "As soon as we can, we'll be husband and wife." He grinned. "Now, go get your stuff. I'll be waiting for you."

She spun around and ran.

The vision faded and I opened my lids to find the white ghostly vision of my dead twin sister. I gasped then shook my head.

"Hey," I said after catching my breath.

"I'd seen that you were having a vision and I didn't want to interrupt."

I slipped on my gloves, returning the pins to the box and gave her a run down on the vision.

"Either of those two, ring a bell?" Steph asked.

"Nope. They wore bell-bottoms and outfits like were common in the seventies. I'm thinking since the pins themselves are probably from around the fifties or sixties, the girl didn't look a day over sixteen. She should be around her late forties or early fifties by now, don't you think?"

"If she got them from her mom, ran off to have a kid, then never returned? Don't know how you're going to figure this one out."

I replaced the box in my drawer and grinned. "First stop, Marnie, since she'd have newspapers back then which might say something, or perhaps she's heard about any rumors of unwed mothers who suddenly left town back in the day." I leaned forward. "Especially since this girl looked like she'd be close to Marnie's age."

"What about the diary?"

"If I don't have a name, looking in Aunt Caroline's diary might not work." I leaned back. "One step at a time, eh?"

"Yep. Call if you need me," she said before evaporating.

I frowned when she left. *I'm afraid of not needing you.*

Chapter Three

"The hairpins belonged to a young pregnant woman?" Maggie asked the next morning while we sat in our office in the store.

Scanning the monitors and noting no customers in the store, I nodded. "She and her boyfriend, I'm assuming, decided to pawn them for money to run away."

She cupped her chin in one hand humming. Sounds of the early morning thunderstorm reached us in the small room.

"I only know she called him Brian, which isn't very helpful."

Maggie sat back. "What if we can get our hands on some yearbooks from that time?"

A loud boom shook the walls making Maggie and I squeak, then laugh. I shook my head.

"Gotta love these storms."

She lifted one corner of her mouth. "Only bad thing is tourists don't like going out when there's storms. Weatherman says it's going to be like this all week, which means it'll be slow as heck in here," she said, then tipped her head to the side. "Which will

give me time to add a few more items to our website." She put her hands on the keyboard and typed a few words. "Ugh. Internet is slow this morning." She faced me and continued. "You'd be able to pick out their faces from a yearbook, right?"

"True. But only if they made it through the year to get their pictures done. What if they didn't? They wore coats, which tells me this happened during the winter months. How early are high school pictured done?"

"Depends. The school here is hit and miss. One year it was early in the year, the next they didn't do them until after Spring break," she shrugged, then glanced at her computer screen. "Since we don't have a specific year, I can't find out when the pictures were done for school."

"Back to Plan A," I said.

She leaned forward. "What's Plan A?"

"Hit up Marnie and her newspapers."

"She'd be about the same age as the kids in your vision. She might know them."

"That's what I was thinking. If nothing else, she'd be able to tell me when the school pictures were done and if I should go that route in figuring this out," I said.

"Smart," she waved a hand at the monitors. "It's slow in here with the weather like it is. You could go now."

"I will let you know what I find out," I said grabbing my yellow rubber raincoat and boots. Slipping the gear on, I spun in a circle. "How do I look?"

"Like one of those advertisements for a rainy day. You don't like umbrellas?"

"They're fine in light rain. But wading out into the storm?" I waved toward the ceiling. "I'm going to stay drier in this outfit."

"Good luck,' she called out as I walked toward the back door. Once outside, I finished snapping the top of my raincoat and sloshed through the rain down toward Andy's street. Good thing everyone I cared to see lived within a short distance from Trinkets. As the wind picked up and whipped raindrops against my face, I dipped my chin. Water splashed on the ground while I made my way to Marnie's house.

****

"You think she's around my age, huh?" Marnie asked while handing me a small towel and setting my iced tea on the coffee table sitting between us in her front room.

I towel dried my hair while looking through the glass of her front bay windows. The storm raged on outside, splattering her windows with water while the wind made the trees lining her front walk sway in a silent tandem with each other. I spun around and sat on the old upholstered couch. "I do. I'm thinking in the last year or two of high school. Maggie suggested looking at yearbooks from that time."

Marnie held up a finger. "Wait a minute. Let me think." She tilted her head to the side. "You said she and her boyfriend left town suddenly?"

"I'd think so, since they arranged to slip out before her father got home from work and they're running away without telling anyone," I said.

"You know, I think I might know who it is. You said you'd recognize her face if you saw a picture?" She asked.

I nodded and she jumped up.

"Stay here, let me grab something," she said rushing out of the room.

I sipped my tea while leaning back on the couch and waited. Within minutes, she returned with a blue folder. She sat, opening it and flipping through the papers inside. Pulling out a newspaper clip, she handed it over to me. "Look at that picture and tell me if it's the same girl from your vision."

I scanned the picture first. It's her. Scanning the headline, I gasped. "Missing girl?" I asked glancing at Marnie.

"Is it her?"

"I think so. This isn't a good picture of her and in the vision, her hair is short. But she looks very close to her. "What's this girl's name?"

"Debra Haygood went missing during my junior year of high school. Her disappearance shocked everyone. No one knew why and I think that was what got me into investigating things. It's the first 'mystery' I investigated on my own," she said using her fingers to indicate quotes around the word mystery.

"She's the Haygood's daughter?"

Marnie frowned. "Yes. But I never heard anything about her being pregnant. You sure you got that in your vision?"

"Yes. The girl was pregnant because the boy, Brian somebody convinced her to sell something for money, so they could run away and raise the baby. He said something about her parents wanting her to give the child up for adoption."

Marnie shook her head. "I don't know if it's her then. I can't see the Haygood's forcing their only child to give up her baby."

"Especially in that time. I mean, teen pregnancy wasn't unheard of."

"Nor was it the norm. In this town back then?" She grimaced. "I could see it happening to avoid a scandal. Mr. Haygood would have avoided that at all costs. But not Mrs. Haygood. She loved her daughter and spoiled her rotten. It wouldn't make sense for her to leave without telling her mom, at least."

"What if she was afraid of her dad? If he demanded she give up the baby, would Mrs. Haygood go against him?"

Marnie shrugged. "I don't really know. But I can't see Debra getting herself in that position."

I sighed. "I can't be sure this is the same girl. You don't recognize this Brian guy?"

"No and it's a common name back then for boys. Did he look older than her? If so, I could grab a yearbook from the school, and you could look."

"I'm wondering something, though. In what way would you not know this kid? I mean, it's not like Petrie's Crossing was a huge town back then."

"You're right. If I don't recognize the name, he's likely not from around here."

"Then it might not be her. Back then, getting from Augusta to here without being noticed couldn't have been easy."

"True. But if it is her, you can't say anything to the Haygood's until you know for sure. I don't think Mrs. Haygood ever got over her daughter going missing."

"Of course, I won't. You know me. Get all the facts I can first, then make trouble." I grinned and Marnie laughed.

Another boom of thunder blasted outside and we both jumped. I rose. "I guess I better get home before it gets dangerous outside with all that lightning."

"I can give you a ride," she offered.

"Thanks, but I like walking." I said before suiting up again. Waving to Marnie, I ran outside and kept up a slow jog all the way home. By the time I arrived, my pant legs were drenched from the run and I shivered while removing my coat and boots. Rushing into the bedroom, I changed into dry clothes and sprawled on the bed staring at the ceiling as though answers might suddenly appear across the painted wall. *Like that ever worked before.*

Chapter Four

I rose from the bed, heading back to my office. Another vision might help clarify things since I had a face now to compare. Going through the routine of lighting incense, candles, flipping on the music, again, I made my way to the chair. Slipped on my gloves and I tugged out the box and lifted the hairpins. Setting them in the center of the desktop, I removed my gloves and lowered my lids, doing a breathing exercise, before lifting the pins into my hands. Holding them, I blanked my mind and waited.

"Brian," Debra gasped. "Mr. Green gave me over a hundred dollars for them," she said sliding into the passenger seat of his car.

"Let me hold onto the money," he said lifting out a hand toward her. She plopped the wad of bills into his hand, then turned up the heater.

"It's cold in here," she said before putting on her seat belt.

"It'll warm up once we get going," he said placing the car in gear and driving up the back alley behind the pawnshop. "This is it, baby. Our lives begin now."

Debra beamed holding her hands across her belly.

The vision faded and I dropped the pins back into the box. Leaning over, I grabbed Aunt Caroline's diary out of the drawer which housed the box. Now that I had a name, I could search in the worn writing filled pages for more information. I flipped through several pages until my gaze caught sight of the name Debra. Setting the book on the desk, I turned back a few pages and started reading.

"Poor Gladys. My heart breaks for her. I don't know what I might do in her shoes. My life has always been about making things as best as I could for my sweet Beth, then for little Lisa. How awful to have your only child go missing so soon after learning she's carrying your first grandchild? Waiting to hear of any news from the police must tear her apart. If my Beth didn't need me close, I'd be out there with the rest of Petrie's Crossing residents searching for the girl. I gathered the courage to inquire if Gladys thought Debra might have run off with the baby's father. She adamantly denied anything of the sort could be possible. Yet, I wonder.

It is a time like this which brings back memories of my own escape. Although Mother knew of my plans to leave, Father had no idea. Had they contacted the authorities to look for me? I shudder to think if I'd been caught and returned to the place I was raised.

I've spoken to Gladys several times and have never heard anything to convince me her husband remotely resembles Father. Surely, he'd support his daughter in her choices, wouldn't he? I am saddened by the thought of judging others. However, if they are responsible for her disappearance, I'd never forgive them. My only hope is Debra followed my own path in running away to provide a different life for her babe. I can only wish them luck if that is the situation. If not, no. I cannot allow the possibility to take root in my mind that such a sweet girl would be harmed or in danger. I will pray for my dear friend and her daughter."

I flipped through until near the end when I saw Gladys' name again.

Gladys wept in church again today. Why the pastor felt the anniversary of Debra's disappearance should carry a sermon on obeying parents I'll never know. I wept with her over the cruelty he inflicted with his words. To even infer Debra Haygood should suffer the consequences of her actions in disobeying her parents' wishes is deplorable. I spoke to my friend after the services concluded. It appears she has accepted the fact that she will never see her daughter again. I truly believe she has been convinced her daughter is not alive and her grandchild lost to her forever.

I closed the book, removed my gloves and wiped the tears which fell down my cheeks. No doubt the pins belong to Mrs. Haygood. But how is this going to affect her? How can it help her with returning the items her daughter sold to leave? I groaned aloud.

"Well?" Steph asked appearing instantly beside me.

"I know who the pins need to be returned to."

"Cool."

"No, not cool." I relayed everything I'd found out so far.

"Ouch. Returning those might cause more pain," she said.

"I'm afraid of that. But would finding out her daughter left of her own free will and was not kidnapped or anything help?"

"It might. It's got to be better than believing her daughter is dead."

"I don't know if she's alive," I snapped.

Steph flickered. "Don't get defensive."

"I'm not," I said then sighed. "My visions don't confirm living statuses. We both know that."

"True. Let me rephrase then. Isn't it better to know her kid ran away than got killed?"

"You're right. Sorry."

"You could ask Officer Rick to help."

I shook my head. "Not yet. Marriages are public records. I'm going to see if maybe they did get married. Plus, I might be able to check to see where her baby was born."

"Um, you're forgetting something."

I glanced at her, "What?"

"Where you going to look? Did your vision indicate where those two ran off to, or you going to search all of Georgia only? What if they went west, or east?"

Drat. "Right again. I don't know where I should search." Leaning back in my chair, I rubbed my hands together. "Okay, at sixteen, we don't really think our world exists beyond what's close to home. At least, I didn't. If I were running away, I think I'd stay close," I paused.

"Go on."

I continued. "Aunt Caroline didn't even leave the state. She simply found some small town her parents wouldn't think of going to, in order find anonymity."

"Yeah."

"So, I think I'm still going to keep the search within the state first. If I'm lucky, they didn't cross the border."

"Sounds like a plan."

"If nothing pops up, I'll ask Rick for help." That's what I'll do. Keeping that in mind, I put away the

diary, closed the drawer and checked the time. "I'll deal with this tomorrow. Mitch is due home soon."

"That's my cue to take off," Steph said fading out.

Chapter Five

Late Thursday morning, I slogged through the wet streets and made my way into Trinkets to find Maggie in the manager's office. I scanned the walls and frowned.

"Andy finished this over a month ago and I put up a picture. You going to get this place decorated or you prefer bare walls?" I asked.

Maggie grinned. "I'm still considering how I want to fix it up. I called Ms. Michelline yesterday and she's making me a wall hanging."

I sat across from her and lifted a brow. "What kind?"

"Not saying. It's a surprise." She leaned forward, placing her folded arms on the top of the desk. "Stop avoiding the subject and give me the latest in your recent quest."

"Quest?"

She shrugged. "It's the gamer in me. What did Marnie have to say?"

"Well, we found out the girl is Debra Haygood--"

"Like the drugstore Haygood's?" She interrupted.

"Yep. Teen pregnancy and her boyfriend, some guy named Brian made her sell the heirloom hairpins her mother passed down to her for money so they could run off and start a family together."

Maggie leaned back, rubbing her chin. "So, runaways. Wow. I couldn't imagine doing that to my parents, even though I don't get along with them. I still wouldn't be so mean as to run off and not let them know about a grandchild."

"See, this is the thing. Her parents knew she was pregnant, wanted her to give the baby up for adoption and then come back home. Mrs. Haygood wasn't happy about that decision."

"Do you think Debra got hoodwinked by the boyfriend?"

"Hoodwinked?" I shook my head. "Where do you come up with these words?"

"You know what I mean."

"I do and from what Marnie has told me, I truly don't think she was one hundred percent on board with the running away part. I think her boyfriend convinced her they had no other choice if they wanted to raise the baby themselves."

"When you're that young and in love, it's easy to believe things" she said.

"Yeah. Poor girl."

Maggie straightened. "I'm not so sure I'd agree with your 'poor girl' statement. It takes two to tango and from the description of your vision, Debra's arm wasn't twisted to go along. Convinced, yes. But forced? Doesn't really sound like it."

"At that age, convincing someone with pressure is the same as forcing in my mind."

"Hm. Maybe."

"We'll agree to disagree. What's your next move?"

"If the storm hadn't knocked out our power yesterday, I'd planned on searching the internet for birth or marriage records. I wanted to come over and see how we're doing with the egg situation before I delve into that particular rabbit hole."

"The diner is delivering our eggs the Wednesday before the hunt."

"They're only giving us three days to decorate that many eggs?"

She lifted a hand. "Don't freak out. I've already arranged for Andy, Nancy and the kids to come over after lunch on Friday to get started. I'll be here to organize everything, and Nancy will supervise if we get customers. Although, if the weather doesn't clear up and give us at least a week of sun, the Easter Egg Hunt is going to turn into a mud bath for everyone."

"Oh man, that'd be a sight to see," I said then chuckled at the image of Petrie's Crossing kids covered in mud while digging for eggs. "Parents will not be happy."

"It'll be fine, I'm sure. It's like we say here in Georgia. If you don't like the weather, wait a bit, it'll change."

"So true." I stood. "Well, since we're so slow, I'm going to head home and work on my computer for those searches."

"I will be waiting with bated breath for your next reveal," she said in a deep tone.

I winced and left, donning my rain gear before facing the pouring rain once more. *I could only hope I had something to reveal next time.*

****

Once settled behind my desk, I began a search using Debra's first and last names, since I didn't have Brian's last name. In minutes, an old newspaper obituary from 1983, popped on the screen. Oh no. I covered my mouth and read.

"Debra Haygood of Savannah died Monday, leaving behind her husband Brian and baby, Charles."

Her picture looked like one taken in a park somewhere. So, she passed away soon after giving birth? I completed the calculations in my head.

Worse. Poor baby angel died giving birth to her son. Why hadn't this Brian guy contacted the Haygood's to tell them their daughter passed away? Why hadn't anyone thought to check online for obituaries before now? Something didn't make sense. I didn't get anything in my visions of Debra marrying.

"Hey there," Steph said from across the room where her misty form floated above the purple couch.

I glanced her way. "If I lost my kid and thought she might be a runaway, or even if she might be dead, I'd be looking in obituaries every week. Wouldn't you?"

She nodded.

"Then how could the Haygood's not know their daughter is dead?"

"How do you know they don't?"

I slumped in the chair. "I hadn't thought about that."

"But then, if they know, wouldn't Marnie know as well?"

I sat up. "You're right. This doesn't make sense that something as simple as an internet search can confirm if she's alive or not, and that no one thought to look?"

"Got me."

I stared at the screen in front of me. Yep, it was her obituary right there in plain sight. "If I can find it, anyone can. It's not like I'm a tech genius or anything."

"Yeah," she agreed floating over and stopping beside me to look at the screen. "What are you going to do?"

"Absolutely no idea." I rose, walked through her form, shook from the quick chill and dropped onto the couch she vacated. Closing my lids, I groaned. "I'm not telling the Haygood's what I found. I can't."

"They have a right to know."

"I agree. But I'm not telling them. I don't care if I'm supposed to return those pins to Mrs. Haygood. I'll have to figure a way to tell her how I came across them, but I'm steering clear of what happened to her daughter."

"If you can."

"I will, one way or the other." I opened my lids and peered at her. "You think if I tell Marnie, she could tell them?"

"No. You should tell that Officer Rick dude. The Haygood's should hear it from law enforcement and not someone from town."

"You're right. You're right. Dumb idea." I glanced at the time and rose. "He should still be at work. I'll call him and let him know what I found."

"You going to tell him the rest?"

"Do you think it'll make a difference right now? I mean, the most important thing is to let the Haygood's know their daughter is dead and they have a grandson out there somewhere." I heaved a deep sigh. "Well, seems like there's no avoiding this part." I tugged my phone out of my pocket and lifted my gaze toward Steph before punching in Rick's number. "You sticking around?"

She flickered, then frowned shaking her head. "Nope. Sorry, you're on your own with this call. I'm going to go rest."

Perfect. Rest? I frowned and waited for the call to pick up, only to get his voicemail. After leaving a message asking him to call me. I disconnected, slumped in my chair and Harmony hopped on my lap. I stroked her fur, leaned my head back, and closed my lids, forcing my mind to blank. No more visions. Need   rest.

Chapter Six

The ringing of the phone startled me out of my short nap. I blinked owlishly, grabbed the phone and checked the screen. Maggie. Punching the button, I answered. "What's up?" I asked checking the time. Trinkets closed an hour ago.

"I just saw an ambulance over by the drugstore. I think something's wrong with one of the Haygood's."

Stiffening, I closed my eyes. "Any idea which one?"

"No. But Mitch ran over there and stayed after the ambulance left. I'm looking now and can't see him anymore."

"I'll call him and find out what's going on."

"I hope they're okay," Maggie said before disconnecting.

Punching in Mitch's number, I waited while it rang...and rang, before going to voicemail. Hmm. Grabbing my coat, I donned it before grabbing my keys and heading out. Once in the car, I paused before turning on the engine. Where was I going? Shoot. Sitting there, I tried calling Mitch again. He picked up after one ring.

"Hey babe," he whispered. "I can't talk for long. I'm driving Mr. Haygood over to the hospital."

"Is he okay?" I asked.

"Don't know. Mrs. Haygood is on her way over there. Looks like she might have had a heart attack from what the paramedics told us."

"Oh no."

"I'll be home late. I'm going to stick around with Mr. Haygood until we can see his wife."

"Should I come help?"

"Probably not. I'm the closest thing to family they have, so I'll take care of them," he paused whispering to someone away from the phone, then returned. "On second thought, I'll call over and have Kim make a take-out box for dinner. If you'll grab that and meet us at Augusta General, that way I can try to get Mr. Haygood to eat something. I assume they're going to be there at least overnight."

"Absolutely. In fact, let me call Kim and do that for you. I'll see you in a bit."

"Thanks," he said then disconnected.

Hopping out of the car, I ran up the street toward the diner. Once there, I told Kim what I needed, then sat in an empty booth to wait. Tugging out my phone, I called Maggie.

"I hope she's okay. You think you should tell her what you're doing?"

"What? Now? No, not a good idea."

"Why not? If she knows she has a grandchild out there, it might give her something to look forward to. Help her to get through this faster?"

"If she's had a heart attack, she's not going to be in any frame of mind to understand what I'm doing or why. At the very least, she's likely going to have to stay at the hospital overnight. Besides, Mr. Haygood isn't likely to let me talk to her right now. It'd be better to wait and talk to Rick first. Last time I told someone about what I'm doing in the hospital, all hell broke loose."

"True. I don't think Dr. Edwards will ever forgive you for breaking in to see Aurora."

"At the time, I thought it was the only thing I could do to help. No hospital visits for me. I'll have to wait until she's released."

Kim arrived with the bag of food. "I gotta go. I'll keep you posted."

"Thanks," Maggie said.

I disconnected, thanked Kim and ran back to my car. The rain had slacked off enough so the food bag didn't get drenched. Jumping in, I slipped the key in the ignition and headed out. Please let Mrs. Haygood get through this. She needs to know about her grandson. I sighed before turning onto the highway leading to Augusta. In less than an hour, I'd arrived

at the hospital, grabbed the food, and rushed into the emergency room waiting area. Searching, I found Mitch and Mr. Haygood standing near the elevators. I joined them, hugged Mitch and turned toward Mr. Haygood.

"How is she?"

"They're taking her into surgery. They found a small blockage, but if they can clear it, she should make a full recovery."

"Oh, that's a relief," The elevator doors opened, and we entered.

Mitch punched the third-floor button and whispered, "We're heading up to the surgery waiting room."

I nodded. "She's a tough cookie. I'm sure she'll be fine." Mitch gave me a small smile and Mr. Haygood simply stared at the numbers while the elevator rose. When the doors opened again, I followed the two men to the waiting room, sat and reached for Mitch's hand. He held it while we sat in silence. The nearly empty room carried whispers from the family across the way which intermingled with bits and pieces of nurse chatter at the desk near the waiting room. I let my gaze scan the carpet as the memory of the last time I chatted with Mrs. Haygood sprang to mind. I grinned when the image of she and I standing and staring outside the drugstore's glass doors while Dr.

Edwards argued with Officer Rick, accusing Marnie's daughter Chloe of tagging his car. She'd called him a bitter man and mean. The image of the first time I'd met Mrs. Haygood also flashed in my mind. She and her husband entering Trinkets...her looking to buy a new dinnerware set...her husband laughing and giving in to her purchase. He did love her, and it was obvious on his face whenever he looked at her.

A doctor arrived and called out Mr. Haygood's name. Mitch and I stayed in our seats while the doctor spoke quietly, before finally turning and leaving. Mr. Haygood approached us with a small smile.

"He says they were able to clear the blockage, and everything is looking good. She's being moved to post-op now and once she wakes up, they'll transfer her to the cardiac unit."

Mitch wrapped an arm around the older man's shoulders. "That's great news."

Mr. Haygood nodded, then pulled away. "She only needs to be here a few days, then if everything is still working good, she'll get released. I need to sit," he said then dropped in the nearest chair. Mitch sat with him, holding his hand.

"It's going to take a bit for them to get her moved," he lifted the food bag. "I had Kim make you

something to eat. You should eat now, so you can be with her without getting hungry."

"I don't know if I can eat," he said.

"You need to eat, Mr. Haygood. You won't be any good for your wife if you don't take care of yourself. She'd want you to eat dinner," I said.

Mitch nodded. "She's right. Eat and I'll wait with you until she gets a room, okay?"

Mr. Haygood nodded. "You're right," he said pulling out the container.

The scent of food made my stomach grumble loud. I slapped a hand to my stomach and mumbled, "Sorry."

Mitch turned toward me, "You need to get home and eat yourself."

"What about you?" I asked.

"I ate a late lunch. I'm good."

I rose and laid a hand on Mr. Haygood's shoulders, "I'm going to head out now. I'm glad to hear your wife is going to be okay."

"Thank you," he responded before digging into the food.

"I'll be right back, George," Mitch said standing and holding my hand. He walked me to the elevator. "Thanks again for bringing the food. I'll be home later," he said then gave me a quick kiss.

Home. Food. Sleep. No wait...need to call and update Maggie first. As I rode the elevator down, I sighed.

"At least she's going to be okay," Steph said appearing in the elevator like a small white misty cloud.

I grinned then whispered. "Yeah, it's a relief."

"I bet. You good?" she asked.

I glanced around when the doors opened. "Yes," I whispered. She evaporated and I headed outside. Time to get home.

Chapter Seven

"Good news," I announced after arriving at Trinkets late Friday morning. "Mrs. Haygood should be getting released tomorrow."

Maggie clapped her hands. "Oh good. Although, Saturday releases are a pain."

I tipped my head to the side. "What do you mean?"

She shrugged. "It seems when it's time to leave the hospital, the minutes seem to go by like a herd of snails. At least, that's always been my experience."

"Do snails travel in herds?"

She frowned. "I don't know. It's a saying my grandma used to use."

"Hmm. Well, either way, I'm sure she'll be happy to be home."

The bell above the front door jingled and Marnie strode in wearing her working clothes of stained jeans, dirty tennis shoes, and ragged sweatshirt. Summer or Fall, she always wore a sweatshirt when cleaning. I waited for her to join Maggie and I at the counter, although the store stood empty at the moment.

She glanced between the two of us and focused on my face. "I got some information for you," she said.

I smiled. "About?"

She glanced again toward Maggie before returning her gaze to me. I dipped my chin. "Maggie knows what I'm doing and everything you know about me."

"Oh, okay." Marnie handed me a small sheet of notepaper.

Without looking, I lifted my brow. "What's this?"

She pointed to the document now in my hand. "When the Haygood's daughter failed to make contact after a month, that their detective was put on the case. At the time, he worked as a private eye. But when he got on the job, he opened a formal missing persons case on Debra. He'd be the one to follow up with on anything you're wanting for your," she waved her hands in the air, "thing."

"Got it," I said then read the name on the paper. Detective Dashawn Paul. I glanced at Maggie, then frowned. "He's based out of Savannah."

"He is now, that's where he got hired on the force. He lived in Augusta before that. I told him you'd be calling him."

"Why?" I asked.

"Because I worked with him on Debra's disappearance at the beginning and he knows me. He's more likely to cooperate with someone who's been referred to him, rather than a stranger."

"She's right," Maggie said.

"I'll give him a call. Can he be trusted?" I asked Marnie.

"Yeah. He's a good guy," she said then spun around heading out. "I'll catch up with you later. I'm off to clean the building next door."

After she left, Maggie turned toward me. "Why does she keep cleaning old buildings when she has enough money to not work?"

I lifted then dropped my shoulder. "She says it's to keep her from getting bored, now that Chloe is away at school."

"Makes sense," she responded. "So, you going to call this detective?"

"I guess I should. If he's any good, he should already know about Debra's passing and her pregnancy, right?"

"He should," she said.

"So maybe he can help find Mrs. Haygood's grandchild?"

"I bet he could if he's still working the case. But, if he knows about Debra, why hasn't he told the Haygoods?"

"Do we know for certain they don't know their daughter is dead?"

She frowned. "I'd think my grandmother would have mentioned if the Haygood's held any kind of memorial service, since she used to drag me to funerals all the time."

I tipped my head. "What?"

She waved her hand. "I know it's weird. But it was one of my grandmother's things, and the Haygood's would have had one for their daughter, since she grew up here."

"You're right. So, it doesn't make sense if he's a detective and doesn't know she's not living anymore. Or," I gasped then continued, "he's keeping it from them? Would he do that?"

"That would be wrong in so many ways. Besides, what would be the point of holding back that kind of information?"

"Exactly. If nothing else, I can ask him about it. If he doesn't know.... well...he'll know after I talk to him."

Maggie placed a hand on my arm. "You think the time is right to have her know what happened to her daughter? I mean, she's not even out of the hospital yet."

"He doesn't have to tell her today. I want to know if he knows, and if he does, why he hasn't told them.

No need to rush on telling her anything right now. If nothing else, I think she needs time to heal up first."

"I don't know," Maggie said.

"Don't know what?" I asked.

"If you'd gone this long thinking your daughter was alive out there, somewhere, would you want to wait to find out? She has a right to know as soon as someone else knows. Isn't that why you're calling him?"

I nodded. "Yeah. I hate to be the one to tell them, but they do have a right to know."

"I'm going to go call this detective now," I said spinning around and heading into the office.

"I'll wait here in case we get any customers," she said.

I entered our small manager's office and situated myself behind the desk in the comfortable leather chair. Taking a deep breath, I punched in the detective's number in my phone. He answered after the third ring.

"Paul," he answered.

"Detective Paul, my name is Shannon Pryce and I live in Petrie's Crossing."

"Marnie said you'd be calling since you're helping her clear some of her old cases. She really should get her PI license. I'm surprised you reached out so fast."

My stomach clenched. "Listen, I did a simple internet search and found Debra Haygood's obituary," I blurted out.

"What?"

"Debra Haygood died during childbirth according to the timing of the obituary."

Silence.

"Hello?" I asked.

"I'm here," he responded.

"Did you know?"

"No. Sometimes, we get so caught up in looking for leads, we miss the obvious." His voice came across very low and I strained to hear him.

"Will you be notifying the Haygoods?"

"I heard Mrs. Haygood is in the hospital."

"She's getting released tomorrow."

"Listen, I'll tell them, but I finally got a lead on her grandson."

"What?"

"Debra had a boy. I'm tracking him down. I think if I have to tell then their daughter is dead, it'd be nice to follow up with their grandson's information."

I bit my lip. "I don't know. I still think they have a right to know as soon as possible."

"I'll think about it. Thank you for the information, Ms. Pryce, I'll handle it from here."

He disconnected the call and I stared at the phone. That's it? I set the phone down since my hands clenched in preparation to throw the darn thing. I stood and paced the office. That's it? Thank you, click? I found out she'd died, not him and that's all he had to say? It wasn't right. Is that how he made his money? Holding back information like now? Jerk. I dropped back in the chair I'd vacated. Did I have the right to tell the Haygood's? My jaw clenched. They had a right to know now, not another day should go by thinking their daughter was out there alive. I blew out a breath. Dash their hopes? Put them in mourning right after getting out of the hospital? Was that the right thing to do? *Shoot.* I stomped out of the office and noticing no customers in the store, joined Maggie at the counter.

"Well?" She asked.

I relayed the very short conversation and she frowned.

"I'm unsure about what I should do next," I admitted.

"Since neither of us have children, it'd be hard to understand what's right here, don't you think?"

I nodded. "What if I ask Marnie?"

"She's a lot tougher woman than Mrs. Haygood. I think her answer would be to know the truth as soon as possible."

"See, that's the thing." I sighed. "I'm going to talk to Mitch about it."

"Good idea. He knows the Haygood's pretty well. He'll know what to do."

I winced. "I hope so." He might also want me to keep out of it. What was the point of having the vision if I couldn't share it? *Drat it all.*

Chapter Eight

Right before closing, Mr. Haygood arrived at Trinkets. He wore a deep scowl across a face reddened and stoic. I straightened my spine and faced him.

He pointed a finger at me. "I want to know what the hell you think you're doing?" He snapped out.

"I'm sorry, Mr. Haygood, I don't know what you're talking about." *Play dumb.* Keep quiet. I chanted inside my mind a calming phrase. *Stay calm.* "Are you okay?"

"No, I'm not okay," he bit out and shot a glare at Maggie who raised her hands and retreated into the manager's office.

I scanned the store, although I knew no one had entered for hours. I looked everywhere but directly at his face. He's mad about something. What could he know?"

He stomped toward me and stopped less than two feet away. I tipped my head to the side and took a slow step backward, lifting my hands in surrender. "Is there something I can help you with?"

"You can help by keeping your nose out of my personal business."

"Excuse me?"

"I know you've been butting into people's business ever since you came to town. I have no clue why Mitch would give you the time of day. You do nothing but upset the good people of Petrie's Crossing with your nosiness and intrusion into their lives."

What did he know about what I've been doing? "Mr. Haygood, you're obviously upset about something and I wish you'd simply come out and tell me what you're talking about."

"I heard from Detective Paul. He said you called him about my daughter. That's something that happened a long time ago and you digging it up right now is incomprehensible and cruel. My wife," he paused and dropped his shoulders before continuing, "she's not in a good state right now both physically and emotionally and you're trying to stir up bad memories with your nosiness. Why would you do this to her?" He clenched his fists. "My wife has been nothing but kind toward you and this is how you repay her kindness?"

"Mr. Haygood, I would never do anything to hurt Mrs. Haygood."

"Except butt into our business like this?" He accused.

"I don't know what Detective Paul said to you--"

"He said you were asking questions about our daughter's case. That was enough for me." He pursed his lips and lowered his voice causing icy tendrils to crawl up my spine. "Stay away from me and my wife. Stay away from this case. Leave us alone. You are no longer welcome at my house. In fact, I strongly suggest you find another place for your pharmaceutical needs as well."

I gasped. "Mr. Haygood, please."

"No! I mean it. Stay away," he spit out, then spun around storming out of Trinkets.

I stood there with my jaw dropped and blinking, then tensed. Jerking my phone out, I began punching in the detective's number, when Maggie's hand whipped around and grabbed it away from me.

"What are you doing?" I asked.

She shook her head. "Never call anyone when you're upset. Grandma's rule." She tucked my phone in her pocket.

"He told Mr. Haygood I called," I said.

"I don't think he should have done that. Marnie said you could trust him, but now I'm wondering that if so much time has passed, he's changed."

"Obviously, he has." I hugged my middle. "I really didn't mean to upset him."

"I know," Maggie said wrapping an arm about my shoulder. "It'll be fine. He's stressed right now, but he'll cool down. He's a really nice guy."

"I know," I mumbled.

She patted my shoulder and stepped away. "Listen, it's closing time. Go on home and chill. Talk to Mitch about what happened and then maybe call that detective back, if Mitch agrees."

"Good idea," I said. "I'll catch you tomorrow." I grabbed her in a quick hug. "Thanks."

"Anytime," she said.

On my way home, I glanced at the bright blue sky with small puffs of clouds rolling and moving as though to their own private melody.

"You're going to trip over something if you keep walking that way," Steph's face appeared above me blocking out most of the clouds.

I blinked and dropped my gaze to the ground. "I don't understand some people."

"It's because you're not like them that you can understand them."

I relayed today's events. "Why would that detective call and tell Mr. Haygood what I was doing? He knows Mrs. Haygood isn't due to be released until tomorrow."

"No clue."

"He won't tell them their daughter is gone, but he'll gladly tell them I'm poking into their business. I don't like his methods."

"Me either."

"I wonder if Rick knows him," I glanced her way. "Think he does?"

"If he was a local private eye, he might. Why?"

"I wish Rick would call me back so I can tell him everything after I talk to Mitch. Maybe he can help shed some light on this sticky situation."

"With what? It's not his case. He doesn't seem like the type to step on another officer's toes."

"Even if that officer is holding back important information?"

"Were you there during his conversation with Mr. Haygood?"

"No, but--"

"Wait a minute. Did you ask Mr. Haygood if he knew about his daughter?"

I gasped. "No. Of course not."

Her ghostly form shrugged. "Then for all you know, they already know about their daughter. That detective could've called to tell Mr. Haygood his daughter's gone, leaving it up to him to tell Mrs. Haygood. He could have told him you only supplied him with the obituary information."

"But, why would he decide to tell Mr. Haygood right after telling me he wasn't going to say anything?"

"Who knows?"

"I don't know."

"Maybe it's not for you to know."

"Whose side are you on?" I asked.

"The Haygood's. It's their daughter's death and their business on how they choose to handle it."

"I never said I wanted to tell them about their daughter or how to handle it."

"Didn't you?"

I paused mid step and pursed my lips, before shaking my head then continued walking. "No, I didn't. I only want to return the hairpins. That's it."

"Then focus on how to return them, not on how the Haygood's are going to find out about their daughter."

"I thought that's what I was doing."

"I know," she whispered then disappeared when I arrived home.

After entering, I checked the time. Two hours before Mitch was supposed to be home. Harmony meowed from somewhere in the back of the house. "I'm home," I called out, heading toward my office. She arrived within minutes, curling herself around my ankles. I sat on the couch and lifted her into my arms.

Nuzzling her neck, I let her purrs fill my ears while I stroked her soft fur. "How are you doing?" She continued purring, nuzzling my neck for a moment before crawling onto my shoulders and proceeding to lick at my hair. I sat there with my lids closed. "I washed my hair this morning. I don't need it washed again." Harmony continued licking with her rough tongue pulling at my hair. I sighed and leaned back, dropping my head on the back cushion. Harmony hopped down and curled against my leg. Within seconds, her soft snoring filled the room. I let the events of the day flicker in my mind for a moment before pushing them out. Relaxation time. Inhaling deeply, I filled my lungs then slowly released the air.

Chapter Nine

Harmony hopped off my chest when the front door opened, and her meowing echoed through the hallway. Mitch's soft voice of greeting the traitorous cat reached me as I rolled off the cushions. Striding straight to his arms, I wrapped myself around his strong shoulders and held him tight.

"Hello there," he whispered in my ear. "I love coming home to you."

I hummed, giving him a quick kiss on the neck, while his arms came about me. Ignoring Harmony weaving herself between our feet, I lifted onto my tiptoes and planted a kiss on those delicious lips of his. The taste of oregano mixed with tomato titillated my tongue. We stood there quietly, kissing with slow sensual movements that made my body hum with desire. Suddenly, my stomach growled loudly causing Mitch's chest to rumble with laughter. I leaned back wincing.

"Sorry, I guess I'm hungry and you taste good, so that doesn't help," I explained.

He grinned, as he took my hand and led me toward the kitchen. "Come on, I'll fix you something to eat."

I grabbed the stool at the counter, watching while he pulled out eggs, cheese, and ham. He flicked his gaze at me raising a brow, "Omelet sound good?"

"Absolutely," I responded while my stomach growled again. Ignoring it, I leaned my arms on the counter.

"So," he said turning on the stove and breaking eggs in a bowl. "Tell me about your day."

"You sure you want to hear? It might upset you."

He chuckled then nodded. "I'm learning not to get upset at your revelations. You worry enough for both of us," he said, pointing a spoon in my direction. "Spill," he ordered.

"Well, I ended my day upsetting Mr. Haygood," I announced, then related the events of the day including my call to the detective.

"The detective told Mr. Haygood about your call?" He asked.

"Yes, which I don't understand because if he had known about Debra's death, why hadn't he told them already, when he thought nothing about telling them I called him."

"In his defense, I'm sure as the lead on the case, he'd be required to keep them updated on anything with their daughter's case. Don't you think?"

"Then why not tell them their daughter is dead? I mean, Mr. Haygood didn't act like a man who recently found out his only child is gone."

Mitch broke several eggs into the bowl, added a little cream, then grated cheese into the mixture. "How do you know they don't already have that information?"

I lifted then dropped a shoulder. "I don't, I guess."

"Then?"

"I don't know. Even if he knew, which, I don't think he did. He said he's following a lead on the grandson."

Mitch poured the mixture in the heated pan, before turning toward me. "A grandson? She was pregnant?"

"You didn't know?"

He shook his head. "Mr. Haygood never mentioned it to me. But I'm not surprised he'd leave that part out."

"I think Debra's boyfriend forced her to run away with him."

"She was being sent away by her parents, anyway, right?"

"I believe their intention was for her to give the child up for adoption, then come home. She never did."

Mitch slid the omelet on a plate and set it before me, handing me utensils. I dug in and my belly wept with the oncoming nourishment. After three bites, I paused. "Wouldn't they have given her money to travel with?"

He nodded. "It's not like they didn't have any."

I paused eating, tipping my head to the side. "If that's the case, then why force her to sell her heirlooms just so they could run away?"

Mitch shrugged. "It wasn't enough?"

"They went to Savannah. I don't know where her parents planned to send her, but whatever money they gave her had to be enough to get them a few hours away."

"Did you get the impression the boy wanted more?"

I shook my head, shoveling in more of my omelet. Man, this guy could cook. Mitch let me eat in silence while he wiped the counter down and washed the dishes. In minutes, my plate sat empty in front of me and I frowned. That was fast.

"Next time, try eating slower."

I scowled at him. "I was really hungry."

"I know. Now," he put my dishes in the sink, grabbed a drink, then tugged me off the stool toward the living room. "let's go make out."

"You're trying to get my mind off this thing, right?"

He nodded. "I love your quick mind."

Once we settled on the couch, and before he could turn my mind to mush with his kisses, I leaned back and held up a hand. "I need to tell Rick everything that's happened. He should know how to handle this detective, right? I don't want the Haygoods to know right now, what I'm doing."

"I agree. You need to let Mrs. Haygood get home and settle down first. Might not even need to tell them if Rick can relay your information to that detective for you."

"He could keep me posted too, regarding the grandson."

Mitch pursed his lips. "Be careful, sweetheart. I don't want George and Gladys to suffer more than they already have."

"I know," I whispered. "I don't want to hurt them, either."

"Tell Rick and follow his advice," he said.

"I will if he ever calls me back," I said then leaned into Mitch, wrapping my arms around his shoulders.

Nipping his neck, I whispered in his ear, "Can we make out now?"

He turned his head and captured my lips in a kiss. Oh yeah. My body tingled as he pressed my back down on the couch and covered my body with his. I wiggled wanting every inch of my body touching his. My pulse picked up and warmth flooded my body. I loved this man, loved the way his body made mine melt, and I loved the way he kissed.

Mitch shifted placing my body on top, tugged off my shirt, then his hands caressed my back and butt. I pressed my hips against his. Sharp claws dug into my back making me yelp and jerk away. Harmony meowed continuing her attack against my bared back. I reached behind me swiping at the fur ball who thought it was time to play. She dodged my hand while Mitch laughed. His body bouncing mine. I sat up, grabbing for Harmony when she jumped onto the floor and scurried away. I frowned at Mitch's laughing face.

"That wasn't funny."

"Yes, it was," he said. He rose, tugged my hand and walked down the hall. "Let's go to bed and shut the door."

"Perfect," I said and stuck my tongue out at Harmony who sat in the hall watching our movements. I spun around quickly shutting the door before she could enter the room. When I turned toward Mitch, he'd shrugged off his shirt and crooked his finger in my direction.

"Shower first, young lady," he ordered, dropping his pants in his wake as he walked into the bathroom, pausing and lifting a brow in my direction.

I crossed my arms. I wanted to go to bed. "I already took one," I said while my mouth salivated at the scene before me.

He winked at me. "Take a second one with me. I dare you," he crooned.

My lips lifted in a grin. So, I did.

Chapter Ten

The following morning, I lay satiated in bed, listening to Mitch shower and get ready for work. My gaze slid to the window as the light gradually illuminated the sky before checking the time. I snuggled farther under the warm quilt, dropping my lids and basked in the mild soreness of my body. Harmony meowed at the door several times before beginning her scratching. I suppose she wants in. I grunted, rolled off the bed and opened the door as she dove between my feet before jumping onto the warm mattress, curling herself near my pillow.

I stared at her, my mouth dropped open as she blinked in my direction once before turning to groom herself. Geez. I made my way to the kitchen, turned on the coffee, grabbed a cup, and then plopped on a barstool to wait. By the time the coffee finished doing its thing, Mitch arrived dressed for work in a white t-shirt and black pants. Dropping a quick kiss on my cheek, he poured us each a full cup of brew, leaned against the sink and after taking a sip, lifted his lips in a wide smile.

"What's your plans for today?"

"I'm going to do some reading in Aunt Caroline's diary, then head on over to visit Mrs. Haygood after making a stop to see Officer Rick, since he hasn't returned my call."

Mitch frowned. "You think that's a good idea?"

"She's getting out of the hospital this afternoon. I'm only going to say hi and get well soon. That's all."

He nodded. "We're setting the schedule to prep the eggs. You got someone to help you decorate yours?" He asked, still wearing that delicious smile of his.

I winced. "Yeah." I straightened my shoulders. "When do I get to the point of not having to do so much for these celebrations?"

"Never," he said then chuckled at my disgruntled expression. "I'll see you later."

He left and I sighed, then padded to my office. Once there, I slipped on my gloves and tugged out the diary. Time to see if Aunt Caroline had anything else to say about the Haygood's. Within minutes, I found an entry.

"I pleaded with Gladys not to send Debra away. I tried, but failed to explain why. How could I reveal my own past without gaining censorship? To be sure, I believe the Haygood's worry about their social standing is like my own parents. Had they been more supportive, I may very well have had the luxury of

being with my sister...my family as I raised my child. I will never understand those who would put their positions above their children's happiness. Gladys told me her husband found a place in Alabama to send poor Debra. Some hospital that takes in unwed mothers and assists in adopting out their children. I truly do not think Debra wishes to part with her child. I spoke my mind and I fear Gladys was none too happy to hear my words. From what she has revealed to me, Debra agreed to do as they arranged, then return here afterward. But, for what? I saw Debra last evening and her eyes seemed to carry such sadness. She is due to travel at the end of the week and I am afraid it will be the last that Gladys and George will ever see their daughter. That I can attest to as I have yet to see my parents in the years since I left...no, ran away. I have often thought about trying to contact Mother, now that I have a child of my own. Yet, I am unsure of her response. Unlike Gladys, who has given her daughter some small means of income, I received nothing. I asked for nothing. I chose my path in life, but Debra does not have a choice if she follows her parents' decision. I cannot dwell on this again as it brings back too many painful memories of my own situation."

I set the diary on my desk, closing the pages. Letting memories of Grandma Brenda flash in my

mind, I wondered why she hadn't been closer to Aunt Caroline. Did her sister's leaving really cause such a rift in the family that Grandma couldn't forgive? In all the years I'd lived with her, not once did I ever see her hold a grudge. It didn't make sense. Sighing, I returned the diary to the drawer, removed my gloves, then leaned back, gazing out the windows where the dawn had cleared the way for gray skies filled with white clouds. Would the sun ever come out? Shaking my head, I rose and headed to shower and dress. Maybe I could try another vision since I didn't get many answers from that detective, only more questions. I paused. Did I really need to know more? Yes. Everything I'd returned meant something to their owners. These hairpins must mean more than confirmation that Debra sold them to run away. How could that be anything but painful to the Haygood's? It wouldn't. Shaking my head, I forced my mind to focus on getting ready for the day.

****

An hour later, I sat in my office once again, inhaling the aromas of the incense I'd lit. The soft sounds of the sea filled the room from the playlist I'd turned on. Harmony lay on her back near the doorway, sleeping. Going through the routine of donning gloves, pulling out the hairpins, removing the gloves, then blanking my mind preparing for a vision, I lifted the pins another time. An image formed of a younger version of the Haygood's sitting in their home talking to a police officer.

"I'm telling you, she wasn't due to leave until this weekend. It's been two days and we don't know where she is," Mr. Haygood snapped.

"You don't think she might have just left early for the hospital?" The officer asked, then winced when Mrs. Haygood began crying. "I'm sorry. I need to ask these questions."

"I understand that officer. However, I'm telling you, she's never left like this before. There's no note, nothing. She agreed to go to that hospital in Alabama and I planned to take her. Her suitcases are packed and sitting in her room. If she decided to leave early on her own for the hospital, why didn't she take her suitcases?"

"Did you look in them?"

Mrs. Haygood dropped her hands from her face. "Look in the suitcases? Whatever for?"

"To be sure they're still packed."

"Why wouldn't they be?" She cried.

Mr. Haygood patted his wife's shoulder. "Sweetheart, he does have a point." He rose. "Let me go check them."

The officer nodded and scribbled in his notebook again before lifting his face and asking another question. "I don't mean to intrude, but, again, I have to ask these questions."

"What is it?" Mrs. Haygood snapped.

"Do you know who the father of her child is?"

Mrs. Haygood's face paled. She lifted her fingers to her lips and nodded.

"I need a name."

She shook her head. "He doesn't live around here and hasn't been to town for several weeks. Debra told me she'd revealed her condition to him, and he left her."

"I'd still need his--"

"One of her suitcases is empty," Mr. Haygood interrupted. "She's removed the clothes."

"George, why? Where would she go?" Mrs. Haygood collapsed, dropping onto the seat cushions of the couch. Mr. Haygood rushed over to her.

"Gladys," he cried then turned toward the officer. "She's not breathing."

The vision evaporated as I gasped, then dropped the pins, slumping and covering my face. *Not good. Not good at all.*

Chapter Eleven

After twenty minutes, I finally found a parking spot near the front entrance of the hospital. Grabbing my purse and the bouquet of flowers I bought on the way, I headed inside. I called Mitch while in the lobby and got Mrs. Haygood's room number. Making my way toward the elevator, I let Mr. Haygood's prior visit sift through my mind. I'd promised to stay away from his wife, but only due to the situation with Debra. Since I was here on behalf of me and Mitch, he shouldn't get upset. I crossed my fingers as I rode the elevator to the floor where Mrs. Haygood's room was located. Please don't let him be upset. I really wanted to see her as a friend and make sure she was okay. I made my way to her room and paused outside the open door, listening. Only the faint sounds of the television came through. If she's alone, this would be easy. I quietly entered the room and found her dressed and packing a bag.

"Mrs. Haygood?"

She glanced up and smiled. "Hello there. I'm getting discharged today."

"I heard. I wanted to bring you these," I handed her the flowers and she lifted them to her face, sniffing the blooms.

"Thank you. They're beautiful."

"They're from Mitch and me. We were sorry to hear about your incident and hope you'll get to feeling better soon." I glanced around the room, found a chair, and sat. "I bet you're excited to get home?"

"I am," she nodded, before pushing her bags aside and sitting on the bed. "George will be here to pick me up in about an hour. I've already signed all the paperwork and I couldn't keep myself in bed any longer."

"I understand."

She peered at me for a moment before speaking. "May I ask you something?"

"Certainly," I said.

"I got this book to read while waiting and recovering," she tugged her overnight bag toward her and pulled out Hank's book.

My hands clenched as my cheeks numbed. I bit my lip. Oh no, did she figure it out? My stomach roiled making me swallow several times while I pressed my lips together and kept quiet, waiting for her to continue.

"I was reading this and it's such a sad story. Have you read it? It just came out a month or so ago."

I forced my head to nod.

"What did you think? I mean, the psychic in this story went through a terrible ordeal, not to mention the poor parents. Do you believe in psychics?"

I swallowed a lump down my throat and nodded again. I couldn't speak.

She lowered her voice, and after glancing toward the door, leaned forward. "I have a situation where I thought I might get some help from a psychic. I'd never considered it before, because George doesn't believe in them. He calls them quacks," she said wincing.

"Oh?" I croaked. Great. He'd never understand my gift.

"Yes," she dropped her gaze and fiddled with the bed covers, then glanced up again. "Do you think that's unwise of me?"

I shook my head. "No. Several people believe in psychic abilities."

"I was wondering if you'd help me."

I stiffened. Help her? Uh oh. "Um, how?"

"Well, you're young and haven't lived here your whole life like me. Would you know how to find one? Or, how to find a good one?"

"Find a good one, what?" Yes, play stupid.

"A psychic. I mean, this would have to be kept between you and I, of course."

Her face flushed, then her shoulders dropped. I coughed. Drat. What to do.

She spoke again, "Unless you think it's a bad idea."

"Oh no, I don't. I'm just not sure what you're wanting to find out. I mean, even the best psychics out there can get things wrong."

She waved her hand. "Oh, I know. I'm only looking for another way to get some information about a situation."

"I see. I can try to ask around for you," I paused and studied her face. She really wanted to do this. "I know there's a place in Augusta...a metaphysical store. I'm sure they have contacts."

She smiled. "Perfect. If you could ask for me? I'm afraid George won't let me out of the house for at least another week."

"I'll ask."

"Thank you so much. You know," she bit her lip then continued. "I always thought there was something special about you."

Nah, she couldn't know. "Oh?"

"Yes, you're a kind person who cares. I really appreciate this. It'll be between you and I, right?"

"Right."

I checked the time. Mr. Haygood can't find me here. I rose. "I'd better let you finish packing and get out of your way. Once I find out something, I'll call?"

She nodded. "Or come by and visit?"

"Sure," I agreed and spun around, heading out toward the elevators. I rolled my head to loosen my stiff neck muscles. If Mr. Haygood ever found out what his wife asked me to do, he'd kill me.

****

Once home, I strode directly to my office and prepared for another reading. The more information I could gather, the better it'd be when I spoke to Mrs. Haygood about her daughter. Could I find where the baby and his father lived? As I held the pins, I blanked my mind waiting for another vision.

A young doctor wearing scrubs stood in a hospital hall speaking to Brian.

"I'm very sorry, but she didn't make it. There were complications during birth." The doctor touched the young man's arm. "The baby survived. You've got a very healthy baby boy."

"I don't want the baby," he snapped.

The doctor jerked back. "But, he's your son."

"I don't want him. In fact, I don't want to...no, that's not true. I'm in shock. Yes, I'll take my son. How soon can I have him?"

"He'll need to stay overnight, at least. Are you prepared to take him home?"

"Yes."

"And the baby's mother?"

"She's dead and I can't afford to bury her or nothin'."

"We have counselors and people who may be able to help."

Brian shrugged. "Okay."

The vision disappeared followed by another.

"I'm telling you he's healthy. You want him or not?" Brian stood with a young couple in a park.

"We do. But I think we need to go through the proper channels of adopting him."

"If they'll let you have him." He glared at the couple.

"Honey," the young woman said placing her hand on her husband's arm. "If we say that Brian is your cousin or brother and turning over guardianship...that would work, right?"

"Yeah, let's do that. You find a lawyer to draw up the papers and I'll sign them."

"What about the baby?" The man asked. "Are you taking care of him?"

"Don't worry about the kid. Call me when you got the paperwork in order, I'll meet you at your lawyer's *office with the baby. You'll get him after you give me the money."*

"You'll sign the paperwork?"

"After I see the money."

Another image quickly flashed of several days later. The young couple and Brian, along with the baby, sat in a formal office signing papers. Brian left the baby, walked outside and after turning the around the corner, pulled out a large wad of bills, grinning.

The image faded, I dropped the pins on the desk and sighed. He sold the baby. How could he do that? Why would he do that?

Chapter Twelve

I spent my time while waiting for Mitch to come home making dinner which combined leftovers and a salad. No way did I like competing with a chef for a meal. Anyway, he rarely ate large meals at home which never affected my appetite.

"You okay?" Steph asked while forming into a more opaque version of me.

I jumped, spun around and scowled. "You scared me."

"Why?"

"I'm not used to you showing up here in the kitchen."

"Oh. Should I announce my arrival with moaning or something?"

I tipped my head to the side and lifted a brow. "Moaning?"

"Yeah, like woo-woo. Or, maybe a whistle?"

"You're reaching," I said, then giggled. "Whistle?"

"Hey, just throwing things out there." She floated across the kitchen and leaned against the counter. "So, what's got you upset?"

I frowned. "I didn't think I was so upset you'd feel it."

"Maybe I'm getting more sensitive to your moods?"

"You're not around much anymore to get a good read on my emotions. Besides, I am a bit upset. This reading...vision, I just had upset me."

"What happened?"

"Look inside my head and I'll replay it for you. It'll be faster and I can work while you look."

"Okay," she said.

I quickly replayed the vision in my mind.

"Ouch. He sold the baby."

"See?"

"Selfish ass."

"I know. Poor Debra and her parents."

"Well, the couple seemed nice enough."

"I thought so too. I hope he was loved."

"I'm sure he was. If you're paying for a baby, you must be desperate, don't you think?"

"Yeah." I nodded. "Okay, so that's a good thing."

"But still upsetting."

I winced. "Yeah."

"Mitch on his way home?"

"Yeah, soon," I said.

"You keeping him posted on everything?"

"Of course."

"Except me?" She asked.

"Except you, as promised."

"Good. Okay, I'm going to head out."

I checked the clock. "We still have time."

She shook her head and flickered. "Not taking any chances."

I blew out a breath as she faded out. I missed our time together. Biting my lip, I spun around and finished preparing dinner. *I'll figure out something.*

When he arrived, I filled two wine glasses, handed him one and we sat for dinner.

"I did another reading today and the vision wasn't a great one," I announced between bites of salad.

"What happened?" Mitch asked.

"After Debra died giving birth to a boy, her sleazeball boyfriend sold the baby."

Mitch paused mid bite. "He what?"

I waved a hand. "He did a private adoption with a lawyer to make it legal, but it was for money. He never wanted the child." I filled him in on how the entire event played out during my session.

"Did the adoptive parents at least look like they were good people?"

I nodded. "They did. Thank goodness they insisted on getting a lawyer to make it legal. But, I'm not sure if that detective down there would be able to figure that out."

"Especially if he thinks Brian kept the baby. He'd be following him, not the child."

"Exactly," I finished my salad and Mitch cleaned the table. "I was thinking about something and I need your opinion."

"What's that?" He asked, rejoining me at the table.

"If I could get closer to where the adoption took place...or maybe try to find the hospital where the boy was born, I could find out more information. Maybe."

"You mean go to Savannah?"

"Yeah. What do you think?"

"Could you guarantee you'd get the information? You're not like a private investigator or anything. You don't have any legal right to the information and likely the hospital, and the lawyer, if you could find him, would be unwilling to cooperate."

I leaned back in my chair. "Then I don't know how else to figure out what happened. I doubt that detective would be able figure out the baby was adopted, don't you agree?"

Mitch shook his head, frowning. "I don't think it's a good idea to go to Savannah. If Detective Paul finds out, he's likely to say something to the Haygoods and that would blow everything up."

"True."

He tipped his head to the side. "You visited Officer Rick. What did he have to say?"

"I didn't catch him at the office. The receptionist said he's been busy with some college students camping out at that old playground they have locked up behind the church?" I shrugged. "I guess the students found a way in."

"Oh. But you'd think he could still call. You leave him another message?"

"I did and he called me back."

"And?" Mitch asked.

"And I haven't got back to him yet," I admitted ignoring the heat in my cheeks.

"Don't you trust him?"

"I do. I don't trust that detective in Savannah. He told the Haygood's I called," I said leaning forward. "What if Rick tells him what I've found out? Then he goes and tells the Haygoods, and it blows up in my face anyway."

Mitch covered my hand with his. "If you trust Rick, tell him everything. He knows about your gift. Tell him your feelings about that detective too. He's a good man and I'm sure he'd figure out some way to get this information passed on without it coming back to you."

"You're probably right. I'll call him in the morning."

"You could call tonight."

"I doubt he's working tonight."

Mitch grinned. "Yes, but you could leave him a message."

"Okay, fine. I'll do it," I said tugging out my phone and punching in Rick's number. The call went to voicemail and I left a message for him to call me. "Happy?" I asked Mitch.

"Absolutely. Now you can stop worrying about it until morning." He rose, tugged me with him. "Let's go find a movie to watch."

So, we did. I pushed away everything about the Haygood's and settled on the couch with my man. Yeah. My man. I giggled and cuddled with Mitch while he found us something to watch.

****

Monday afternoon, I strode into Trinkets and glanced around. No customers were browsing the goods. I followed the sound of Maggie's voice, finding her in the manager's office. I sat across from her and waited for her to finish her call.

"It'll be here, and I'll mark it for hold. Of course," she said into the phone. I couldn't hear the response, but smiled when she disconnected.

"Customer?" I asked.

She nodded. "Yep and she's wanting that Queen Anne Curio Cabinet, we had on the website. She wants to see it in person before making purchase."

"Ah, okay," I said glancing around. "Has Officer Rick been by or called?"

"No, why?" Maggie asked.

"I had a couple more visions and wanted to go ahead and get him caught up with everything I know so far."

She lifted her brows. "You're not going to tell Detective Paul directly?"

"Heck no. He'd run to the Haygood's and then I'd get in trouble again. Not going to happen. I'll wait and let Rick handle it."

She leaned back in the office chair, crossing her arms across her chest. "So, catch me up then."

I told her about my visions yesterday and Mitch's suggestion.

"Smart move," she said.

The bell over the front door of Trinkets rang, and we both rose to meet the customer, but then froze. Mr. Haygood's face flushed dark red, scowled and pointed a finger at me as he got closer.

"I told you to stay away from my wife."

Uh oh.

Chapter Thirteen

I raised both of my hands palm forward. "I didn't do anything."

"You went to the hospital right before she got released. Do I need to get a restraining order?"

I shook my head vehemently. "No, please don't. I only took her flowers and wished her a speedy recovery, that's all."

"I told you to leave her alone."

That's it. I planted my fists on my hips and glared. "She has always been very nice to me. I am not going to ignore her when she could use some cheering up. I agreed not to say anything about your daughter, and I didn't. I consider her a friend and it's wrong of you to not let me continue that friendship."

"I don't care."

"I do. She's a grown woman and if she wants to be my friend, that's her decision. You can't be that mean."

He jerked his head back. "Mean? I love my wife and I want her to get better. She can't get better if she's stressing about the past and things, she can't do anything about."

"Which I just said I never brought up to her."

He pursed his lips. "I'm only trying to protect her."

"I understand. Please know, I would never do anything to intentionally hurt her."

"That's the problem, young lady. You never seem to want to hurt people, but sometimes you do. I've heard things around town. I know better."

My mouth dropped open. What could I say to that? "But--"

"But nothing," he interrupted. "Please respect my request." He spun around and stormed out before I could respond.

I glanced at Maggie who stood there quietly. "Is he right?"

She shook her head. "No. He's heard some things but, obviously not everything. He's only being protective of Mrs. Haygood. Don't let it worry you."

My phone trilled and I pulled it out to check the display. Rick. Punching the button, I answered.

"We need to talk," he said without any greeting and my stomach clenched. Drat it. Had I already messed things up?

"Did you get my message?" I asked.

"Yep. I'll be out of town until Wednesday. Come by the office in the morning and we'll go over everything."

"Okay. Thanks," I said, then disconnected and faced Maggie, "I'm meeting Rick on Wednesday."

"Good. Let's change the subject."

"Yeah, nothing I can do until then anyway," I said.

"How'd your tea date go with Ms. Michelline, yesterday?" Maggie asked.

I smiled. "She seems happier and we had a nice time. In fact, she told me she's making a wedding quilt."

"Oh really?" Maggie grinned. "Guess you need to set a date soon."

"We haven't even announced our engagement. Mitch isn't likely going to want to set a date before announcing that."

"What's he waiting for?"

My face heated. "I asked him to wait."

Maggie's mouth dropped open for second before she closed it. "Whatever for?"

I lifted then dropped a shoulder. "I kind of thought it might be better if some time passed first."

She shook her head. "I'm not understanding."

"Don't you think it'd be better if I lived here at least a year before making a marriage announcement?"

She frowned. "No. I don't think time matters like it did in the past. I mean, it's not like there's a formal

requirement of time. Isn't that kind of old school thinking?"

"Maybe? I don't know. I keep thinking of everyone who lives here and how I'm still being treated by some of the shop owners as a newcomer to town. I thought after a year, I would stop being treated like that and the announcement would go over better."

Maggie tipped her head and stared at me. "I'm surprised that matters to you."

"Why? This is a small town and you know how everyone is."

"I do. But still. Think about it. It's the twenty-first century, Shannon." She sighed. "Very few people our age make a decision based on what people think."

"You think I'm being ridiculous?"

She lifted a hand, then dropped it. "Not ridiculous...okay, maybe a little ridiculous," she said with a smile. "No offense."

"You might be right. I need to stop thinking of myself as an outsider if I want others to stop too. It is stupid. I'll talk to Mitch about it."

"Good. Then we can start planning your wedding, right?"

I held up both hands. "Whoa there, Chica. Don't rush things."

Maggie laughed.

I grinned and continued, "Ms. Michelline showed me the pattern she's using for the quilt. It's called a Wedding Ring. The colors are bold and beautiful, which she says will match us perfectly. I agreed."

Maggie clapped her hands together. "I can't wait to see it. I might have to sneak over there and beg her for a peek."

"Beg is right. She only showed me three swatches and a magazine picture of the pattern."

"She does such beautiful work. I wish I had that talent."

I blinked. "You want to learn how to make quilts?"

"It's a vanishing tradition and I'd really like to try my hand at it someday," Maggie said.

"She's very nice. I think if you just ask her, she'd be willing to teach you."

"Do you think she would? I mean, I don't even know how to sew. I'd need to learn that first."

"If you don' t ask, you won't ever know."

"True. I could learn in my free time. Maybe I could make Grandma something nice for her place?"

"That's a great idea! Tell Ms. Michelline I suggested you ask her."

"I will," she said then hugged me. "You've done so much for me. Thank you."

"That's what friends are for, right?" I asked.

"Right," she said.

Too bad friends couldn't come along and ward off bad   news.

Chapter Fourteen

Wednesday morning, I drove over to the police station to see Rick. As I entered, he stood waiting for me and gestured for me to follow him into his office. I sat in the chair on the other side of his desk and faced him. He settled behind his desk, tugged a folder in front of him and opened it. I remained quiet while he read the pages, turning over several. Once done, he glanced up.

"Okay, so tell me everything you know so far," he said.

"Everything?"

He nodded. "Describe what you've seen in your visions. If your great aunt wrote anything in that diary of hers, I want to hear about that too."

"Okay," I agreed and told him everything, including Mr. Haygood's visits, accusations and threats.

"But even after you were asked to stay away from her, you went to see her?" He shook his head. "You know that wasn't a smart move."

"I went as a friend and didn't say anything about Debra."

He sighed heavily, crossing his arms on his desk, then leaning forward. "I know you mean well."

"I always do, you know that."

He dipped his head. "I do. I also know some of your...attempts to do the right thing do tend to stir up trouble. You can't say that it doesn't, despite your best intentions."

"I know that. But it usually ends up fine."

"Has it ever crossed your mind that these items...trinkets that you return are a bit too convenient to need returning to the residents of Petrie's Crossing?"

"Convenient? No. Considering that all of them passed through Bobby's grandfather's pawnshop. It makes sense each item at one time belonged to someone who lived in town."

He sat back. "How many more items do you have to return?" He asked.

"There's only three that carry a strong energy which I believe need to be returned."

"But, there's more items there?"

"Yes, but the remaining few, in my opinion, are items which hold no meaning...well...not meaning. They aren't significant enough to give off any energy. Likely items pawned for cash from strangers?"

"Hm. what will you do with those?" Rick asked.

"I guess after I return the ones which carry a strong energy, I thought I'd give them to Bobby to put in the shop. That's where they came from, I believe."

"What if they belonged to his grandfather?"

"Well," I said holding my hands palms up in front of me. "I guess, I'll give them to him, and he can decide that, since I don't get anything from them."

"Do you know where the...what did you say...strong energy ones go to?"

I shook my head. "Not yet, because I haven't done any readings on them."

"I see."

"Why?" I asked. What did that matter?

"I'm thinking if you could do a quick check on the remaining items you intend to return, we could get a feel of who is next on your list of recipients."

"And what would that accomplish?"

He pursed his lips. "I'd have some warning of who you'll upset next?"

"I haven't upset everyone I've returned an item to. Sheesh, you make it sound like that's the only thing that's happened with returning these pieces. Everyone I've returned an item to has been helped in some way." I paused to suck in a quick breath, then continued. "Every person has been grateful to get what belongs to them back."

"Eventually, they are."

"What are you suggesting? I simply find out who they belong to, then mail them the item?"

"No, that's not what I'm saying, and I don't think you could do that, could you?"

"No, I couldn't. I need to know why I'm having to return the item before I do it."

"Why?"

"Because if it won't help, why should I return it? That's why I do what I do and check everything out first. Yes, it can get sticky. But, if I can't figure out why I'm supposed to return the item, what's the point?"

"And you're positive you need to return the items."

"Yes. I am. Okay?" I snapped. Why was he questioning me like this?

He lifted a hand. "Listen, I'm only trying to understand what you're doing. This is the town I'm sworn to protect."

"I get that, but it's like you're accusing me of intentionally trying to cause distress to these people when I'm not."

"I'm not accusing you of anything. Don't get defensive here. Remember, I'm on your side."

"Honestly, Rick it doesn't feel that way right now."

"I am," he said picking up a pen and making notes on his tablet. "I've known Paul for several years. In fact, I remember the whole Debra disappearance fiasco. I was young, but I do remember hearing about it. I pulled the case file and reviewed it. He's still the lead detective on it and although you might not agree with his actions, he is a good man trying his best to help the Haygood's."

"How is he helping them by not telling them she's gone? He's letting them believe she's still alive. That isn't helping."

"That much we do agree on. But, like I said, I've known him, and he has to have a reason for doing what he's doing. I don't want to step on any toes here."

"Neither do I." I shrugged. "But I don't like him."

"I got that much. Listen, I'll call him and talk to him about the case."

"And?"

"And I'm going to have to tell him who you are, so he understands why you don't want everything you tell him relayed to the Haygood's."

I stiffened. "He'd do that? Maybe you shouldn't tell him. Do we have to do that?"

He nodded. "I think it's best. He obviously can keep a secret."

I scowled. "True."

"He's a good man. I promise. Let me make a call to him and explain things. You okay with that? I won't tell him who you are or about your past if you really don't want me to. But I think it'd go a long way in helping smooth this situation out."

"You sure we can trust him?" I asked leaning forward. "I trust you."

"I do."

"Okay then. Do what you think is right." I rose. "But if it comes back to bite me in the butt, I'm going to be really mad at you."

He grinned. "It'll be fine. I promise."

I nodded, spun around and left the station. My chest tightened and I inhaled several times while walking to my car. It'll be fine. It has to be fine. *If not, I'm   so   screwed.*

Chapter Fifteen

By Monday night, my nerves were frayed with me with jumping each time my phone rang, the shop door opened, or whenever I spotted Rick driving on patrol through town. He hadn't contacted me since our meeting last Wednesday. As Maggie and I closed Trinkets for the day, I mumbled to myself constantly. "It'll be fine." While I organized the egg-coloring supplies in the break area near the back of Trinkets. Maggie joined me in setting out the egg cellophane wrappers, various dyes, and disposable cups.

"Do you really think we need to dye every egg?" I asked.

"No, just some of them. We'll rotate between wrapping and dying. The twins can do the dying while we help Clara do the wrapping. It'll be fine."

I cringed at her words. "Rick still hasn't called me." I threw up my hands, and then ran my fingers through my hair. "It's driving me crazy."

"I can tell," she said then chuckled. "I'm sure he has it under control and there's a reason for him not getting in touch with you."

"Have you heard anything on how Mrs. Haygood is doing?"

"I snuck over there last night with a casserole," she announced.

I spun around facing her. "Why didn't you tell me that this morning?"

"You've been grumpy."

"I'm sorry. Is she doing okay? Does she look like she's getting better?"

"Yes and yes. She's walking around without help. Moving a little slow, but steady. She seems to be recovering really well."

"Good. I wanted to check on her myself, but--"

"--but you didn't want to face the wrath of Mr. Haygood. I don't blame you. I don't think it's right of him to deny you seeing her." She unwrapped the bulk packaging of paper towels. "Practically everyone else in town has been to see her."

"See? " I shrugged. "I guess I don't blame him." I winced. "It just sucks being ostracized, that's all."

"Yeah, it does." She hugged me. "But I'll keep you posted."

"Thank you for that." My phone rang and I jumped, jerking it out of my pocket and checking the display. Mitch. My muscles relaxed as I answered. "Hey."

"Hey you. Rick called and said he tried calling you earlier but you didn't pick up."

"He did?" I checked my missed calls. Drat it, he had. Why didn't I hear it? "I'll call him back."

"Sounds like a plan. I'll catch you at home. Love you," he said then disconnected.

Aww. He said he loved me first. My belly filled with butterflies before my mind remembered Rick called. Ugh. "I missed a call from Rick," I told Maggie.

She waved me away. "Go on and head out. Fill me in tomorrow."

"Will do," I responded and left. On the walk home, I dialed Rick's number. When he answered, I spoke, "I'm so sorry I missed your call. I've been waiting on pins and needles and can't believe I missed it."

"No worries," he said. "Listen, Paul's in town. I want to bring him over to your place and talk. You free tonight?"

My stomach clenched. Uh oh. "Is it going to be bad?"

"No. Don't freak out. We're going to grab dinner at the diner, then come over. Is that okay? You free?"

I nodded before realizing he couldn't see me. "Yes. Mitch will be home too."

"He knows everything, yes?"

"Of course."

"Good. See you later" he said then disconnected.

Speeding up, I rushed home. Mitch had beat me home and had already started dinner. I joined him in the kitchen, gave him a quick kiss on the cheek and set out plates.

"Rick is coming over after he grabs a bite to eat at the diner. He's bringing Detective Paul with him. He says it's so we can talk."

Mitch paused in the middle of cooking and turned, facing me. "Good news or bad?"

I shrugged. "He didn't really say. He told me not to freak out, so I'm hoping it isn't bad news."

"Well, let's hope so."

"Should I be worried, you think?"

"Nah. Rick is cool. If it's bad, I'm sure he'd have warned you."

"That's what I was thinking."

Mitch plated our food and we sat eating. My stomach, thank goodness, loved his cooking and although squirmy, kept my food down. We ate in silence and I replayed Rick's call in my mind a few thousand times.

"Stop worrying about something you don't know, sweetheart," Mitch said.

"I'm trying not to." I stretched, leaned back in my chair and rubbed my stomach. "At least I have a full belly."

He chuckled as he rose and began clearing. "Why don't you find something to drink and some glasses. We'll set up in the living room."

"Sounds like a plan," I said getting a bottle of nice bottle of Port, four glasses and set them on a tray. Carrying the tray to the living room, I turned on some soft music for background noise and plopped on the couch to wait. Within minutes, Mitch joined me, laying an arm across my shoulders and squeezing lightly.

He leaned in and whispered in my ear, "Want to make out while we're waiting?"

I chuckled then shook my head. "I'd love to." The knock on the front door made me jump. "But they're here." I looked over and checked the time. "That was a fast dinner on their part."

"Likely got something easy or ate fast."

"Who knows," I said rising.

Mitch tapped my arm and pointed toward the couch. "Sit. Let me get it."

"Okay," I said, sitting and inhaling a deep breath before letting it out. *Relax.*

When Rick came into the living room, I rose and shook his hand. "Good to see you."

He nodded and shifted to point to the tall stocky dark-skinned man who stood beside him. "This is

Detective Paul." He waved a hand toward me. "Paul, this is Shannon."

The detective dipped his chin, held out his hand and said, "Nice to finally meet you. Although, I've never worked with a psychic before, so this is all new to me."

I shook his hand and studied his face etched in wrinkles at the edges of his eyes. The tone of his voice made me stiffen. He didn't believe in psychics. *Oh perfect.* He's going to expect me to prove myself. I clenched my jaw. No way. I'd done that before. Not doing it again. *I will not be made to defend my gift to this guy.*

"Let's sit down," Mitch suggested then poured wine. After offering everyone a glass, he sat beside me, holding my hand. "So, what's the news?"

Rick glanced at the detective, who nodded and leaned forward after taking a small sip of wine. "I did some more checking after Rick caught me up on what you...discovered. If I can locate him, we might be able to find out what happened. It seems to me there wasn't any indication Debra had a difficult pregnancy and I did get a chance to talk to her obstetrician. He gave no indication there were any risks. He told me in confidence she did go into labor a month early and he was told she'd fallen down some stairs a few days before she showed up at the hospital."

"I did some checking too," Rick added. "I found a Brian Allman was reported missing by his parents around the same time as Debra." He paused a moment, then continued, "Actually, he left home nearly a month before his parents reported him missing. We don't know where he was staying. I did find a picture of him." he tugged out a photo from his jacket pocket. "Mind looking at this and tell me if it's the same guy from your visions?"

Paul snorted and tried hiding it with a cough. I scowled at him, before taking the picture. I glanced down and gasped. It was him. I handed it back to Rick, nodding. "That's him. He's the father of the baby."

"Makes sense. I called Brian's parents after we talked and went to see them. They mentioned he'd been travelling outside of Augusta to see a girl, but he never told them her name."

"So, he lived in Augusta then?"

Rick nodded.

"We ran a background check on him." He frowned, glanced at Paul who nodded before he continued. "He had several violations as a minor and a couple after he turned eighteen."

"What kind of violations?" Mitch asked.

"Petty theft type of things. Nothing violent. But his parents said he dropped out of high school in the eleventh grade, hung around a bad crowd and got into drugs."

I stared at Rick. "That's not good."

"Likely he got Debra hooked too. It could be what caused the early labor," Paul interjected.

I scowled at him. "She wasn't into drugs."

"How could you know? Your visions prove that?" He smirked. "Drug addicts can hide their addiction from most people."

"From what I've learned from people in town," I faced the detective, "and from my visions, she never behaved as though addicted nor said anything about drugs. In fact, I'm surprised Brian was into them as his behavior didn't appear as one struggling with addiction."

"And you would know this how?" Paul asked.

What a jerk. "Because I'm not stupid? I've seen and read enough to know when it looks like someone is jonesing for their next fix."

Paul shrugged and Rick frowned.

"Did anyone clarify what kind of drugs he was into?" Mitch asked. "Marijuana was deemed very bad back then and likely that's all he was into. My cousins would have told me if there was a harsher drug issue in Augusta as many of them grew up there. I think I would have heard about it growing up."

Rick nodded. "I don't think that matters right now. All we do know is that this kid had some issues prior to talking Debra into running away with him."

"I've also agreed to check with some of my contacts in the legal field regarding who might have handled private adoptions around that time too. I'd prefer to go to the Haygood's with information about their grandchild when I meet with them next." He rose. "I think we're done here." He turned to Rick. "I need to head out."

Rick glanced at Mitch, "Can you give me a ride back to the station so Paul can go ahead and leave? I'd like to talk a bit more, if that's okay?"

"Of course," Mitch said.

"Sure thing," Paul said. "I'll catch up with you later." He strode out the door without even saying goodbye.

Yep, he's a jerk.

Chapter Sixteen

The following Friday as we worked in the shop, I approached Maggie while she retagged several clothing items. About a dozen customers wandered around the store chatting and checking out the items. I glanced around and no one appeared to need help, so I tapped Maggie on the shoulder. She glanced at me and raised a brow.

"So, I told you Rick and that detective came over Monday night."

She nodded. "Yep and that he was a jerk. But you never explained why you thought that."

"In my life experience dealing with non-believers of the metaphysical, it's been easy to get a feel for them," I shrugged.

"What do you mean?" She asked with a confused expression on her face.

"They tend to be short in their questions, disregard or, worse, argue with your answers. Mainly, they come across very skeptical. I don't think he believed in my gift and I got the impression he thought I was more like an amateur detective, or nosy."

"But Rick believes you," Maggie said.

"Yes, he does."

"And if he's a friend of Rick's, he has to respect that, right?"

"You'd think. Unless he thinks Rick is being bamboozled by me."

"Bamboozled?" She grinned. "I haven't heard that word in ages."

"Well, you know what I mean."

"I do. I still think you need to trust Rick in knowing who can be trusted and who can't. He's never steered you wrong in the past."

"No, he hasn't." My phone rang and I pulled it out. "Speak of the devil," I mumbled.

"Rick or the jerk?" She asked with an arched eyebrow.

I smiled. "Rick," I waved and walked toward the back, break area so I wouldn't be disturbed. "Hey Rick," I said.

"I heard from Paul," he announced.

My stomach tightened and I squeezed my lids close. "What did he say? He doesn't like me."

"He's too close to retirement to disregard anything that will help him close this case. It's the only one that has stuck with him since his early days on the force."

"Now I feel bad thinking he was just being a jerk."

"He doesn't believe in psychic phenomenon, but he'll believe anything that will help him on this particular case. Believe me on that. Anyway, I didn't call to talk about his personality."

"Fine. Sorry."

"No, I'm sorry. I don't mean to snap. I wanted to update you as I'm about to head out of town for a couple days."

"What's going on?" I asked crossing my fingers for good news.

"Paul located Brian Allman. He's currently serving time in prison for burglary. But he also got information from a lawyer friend and with the birth certificate, he was able to find out who adopted Debra's son. The bad part is the boy's parents died in a boating accident a couple years ago. So, Paul is handling this with kid gloves. He got a social worker friend of his to go with him."

"Go with him where?"

"To meet with the Haygood's grandson. He's married now and living in Tennessee. I'm going to be joining them since I know the Haygood's. We're hoping he'll agree to meet them or at least contact them."

"Oh, Rick, that's great news. Can I ask what the boy's name is?"

Silence.

"I promise not to say anything to anyone. Not even Mitch, please?" I asked.

"I suppose it won't hurt to tell you. They named him Grant."

I grinned. "That's a good name."

"I gotta go. I'm hitting the road this afternoon."

"Will you tell me what happens with the meeting?"

"If I can. I won't promise anything."

"Okay. I understand."

"You have helped though. Remember that."

"I will," I said disconnecting the call, then staring out the window. Please let him be willing to meet the Haygood's. It would really help when I return the pins. *Ugh. I'm such an optimist.*

Chapter Seventeen

I arrived at Trinkets late Wednesday morning and found the shop full of customers...again. Every day since last week, we'd been busy. Maggie finished ringing up a sale, grinned at me, then pointed to the group near the toy section. I nodded and headed over to assist anyone who might need it while scanning the small group of teenage girls sifting through the clothing racks. Busy is busy. Good.

"Can I help you find anything special?" I asked the young couple checking out the dolls where Clara had sweet-talked Nancy into buying. They smiled in unison, "We're looking for something special for our niece," the woman replied.

"Nothing too expensive, but she is going to be turning ten soon," the man added.

"You'll find the most expensive collector items on the top shelf, the pricing values go down as you go down the shelves. The least expensive are on the bottom where little hands can get to." I explained.

"Perfect," the woman said and chose one from the second to last shelf. "I like this one."

"Very good choice," I said holding out my hand. "I'll wrap and ring this up for you."

"Thank you," they said in unison. Aw. Maybe someday Mitch and I will be able to do that after we're married. A warmth flooded over me. Yeah, I'm a sap.

After finishing their sale, Maggie strode over. "We've been like this since I opened."

"Wow. You know next month will mark a year since I got here," I said. "Things have really been great."

"Enjoy it because tourist season will die down around the middle of June. It always does."

"That's fine with me. We can recoup and replenish our stock."

My phone rang. *Mitch.* I answered. "That detective and Rick are on their way over to the Haygood's place. I saw them when I stepped out back to meet the delivery driver," he said immediately.

"Oh? I wonder what's happening."

"I don't know, but they weren't alone," he lowered his voice. "There was a young man around our age with them."

My heart beat hard against my chest. "Do you think it's their grandson?" I asked.

"Don't know," he said, and someone yelled in the background. "I gotta go." He said.

I frowned and pocketed my phone. Rushing toward the front window of Trinkets, I peered out and over toward the Haygood's drugstore, since their home butted against the back part of the building. Sure enough, Rick's patrol car sat out front. Drat.

"What's going on?" Maggie whispered beside me.

"Mitch called and said Rick, that jerk detective and a young man our age showed up at the Haygood's."

"That's all?"

"He had to go, someone needed him. Besides, it's not like he'd have gone over there to find out."

"True. Mr. Privacy at his best. I'm surprised he even called to tell you that much."

I grinned. "Me too. Maybe I'm rubbing off on him?"

She shrugged. "Might be." She continued staring out the window. "We can't see anything from here. How are we going to find out what's going on?"

"No clue. It has to be their grandson."

"I agree," she said.

The back receiving doorbell chimed and we both spun around. Bobby waltzed in with four boys following with cases. I frowned and glanced at Maggie.

She clapped her hands. "All our eggs are here," she said before rushing toward the guys. "I just recounted to make sure we had enough supplies."

Oh great. One hundred boiled eggs to decorate. I joined them while Maggie made room in the small fridge sitting in our break area.

"Will they all fit in there?" I asked.

"They will," she said.

"Well, little lady, I can't wait to see how you do with your batch," Bobby said winking.

"Me either," I responded turning toward him. "You decorating any?"

He laughed making his cheeks red and lifted his hands. "Oh no, last time I did it, I got in trouble, so I don't get to decorate no more."

I frowned. "How'd you get into trouble?" Maybe I could do something like it to get out of doing this next year.

Bobby shook his head. "Nope, not telling. I made a promise to the Mayor never to reveal what happened so no one else uses it as an excuse not to do their part. You got this. Nancy told me that Andy's family is pitching in and helping so you'll be fine."

"Some friend you turned out to be," I said with a smile.

"I know. Well," he said patting me on the shoulder. "Good luck." I scowled as he sauntered out with the boys following him.

"I'll call Andy and we'll get these done on Friday. I think we'll only open half day, so we have the whole afternoon and night to decorate. That'll give the eggs all day Saturday to set before the hunt on Sunday."

I tipped my head to the side. "Um, listen. We don't have to hide them too, do we?"

"Oh no, thank goodness. Those who aren't decorating get that job."

My shoulders relaxed. "Oh good. Then, I guess we'll do this Friday."

"Yep," Maggie said before glancing behind me. "Oops, got someone at the counter."

"I'll get it," I said spinning around. Let her figure out how to fit all those eggs in that small box.

****

Later, as we closed and straightened racks, Maggie called over from across the shop. "I'm thinking maybe I can take another casserole over to the Haygood's and try to get the scoop on what happened today?"

"I don't know. I'm really thinking maybe we should wait until after Sunday."

"We could," she said.

My phone rang and not recognizing the number, I answered. "Hello?"

"Shannon? It's Gladys...Haygood."

"Mrs. Haygood, how are you?" I asked waving at Maggie who ran over to stand next to me. I put the phone on speaker. "I'm sorry I haven't visited, but Maggie told me you're doing much better."

"Yes, I'm doing very well." She lowered her voice, "I can't talk right now as George is in the other room. But I truly want to see you. I need to talk to you about something important."

"Is it about what you asked me to do?"

"No. No, I don't need that. But George is going to be working the drugstore tomorrow all day. He got behind on the paperwork. It'd be the perfect time for you to come over."

"What if he comes home or sees me walk over? I don't want to cause any more trouble," I said. Maggie shrugged and I ignored her.

"You won't. I told him I wanted you to visit and that is my choice. I just don't want him to overhear what we talk about, is all."

"If you're sure?" I said.

"Yes, please."

"Alright. I'll be there after lunch?" Maggie mouthed morning. I shook my head. "Trinkets has been really busy in the mornings."

134

"That's perfectly fine. In fact, I have so much food here, a lot of it will go to waste if someone doesn't help eat it. I'll provide lunch."

"Sounds good to me. I'll see you tomorrow."

"Thank you, I'll see you then." she said then disconnected.

I raised a brow at Maggie. "I wonder what she wants to talk about?"

"Who cares, you can get the scoop from her too. Listen, if that was her grandson that showed up with Rick, then maybe it'd be a good time to give her the pins too?"

I gasped. "You're right. That'd be the perfect time."

"Great. Let's get this place straightened up so we can both go home."

I chuckled. "Race you?"

"Go!" She yelled, running over toward the dish section and organizing as fast as she could move.

I laughed running over toward the clothing racks. *Watch this.* I raced through the clothing, while considering how to tell Mrs. Haygood about the hairpins. *It was time for her to have them back.*

Chapter Eighteen

I knocked on the back-door entrance of the Haygood's home, then rubbed my sweaty palms against my jean clad thighs while taking in deep breaths. Tapping my pocket where the pins sat wrapped in cloth, I waited. The distant sound of slow-moving footsteps reached me through the door only moments before it swung open and Mrs. Haygood stood there with a small smile.

"Come on in," she said waving me in.

"Hello. How are you feeling?" I asked once I entered and faced her.

"Much better now that I've been home." She preceded me down the hallway. "Come into the dining room. I made hot tea, is that okay?"

"Yes, that's perfect."

"Good. Good. Doctor's orders include reducing my intake of coffee. Although," she chuckled, "I do miss my coffee."

We sat at her dining table which held a centerpiece of a large bouquet of flowers. I glanced around and checked out the floor to ceiling china cabinet, filled with various sets of Corelle vintage

dinnerware. I pointed to them. "I see you do have a nice collection there. I'm glad Trinkets helped."

"I just love your shop. George puts up with me buying so much. He knows how much it means to me," she said pouring us tea. She slid my cup to me, then the plate of sandwiches. "Please eat."

"Thank you," I said filling my own plate. Taking a bite out of one, I nodded. "Very good."

She sipped her tea and smiled while I ate. I quickly downed several triangle sandwich bites, before washing them down with my own tea. Then I glanced at her. "You wanted to talk?"

She cleared her throat first. "Yes. Well, I'm not sure how to begin," she lifted her hand and tucked a stray piece of her loosely bound hair behind her ear.

"Mrs. Haygood--"

"Gladys, please," she interrupted. "I'd like you to call me Gladys."

I dipped my head. "Gladys, begin anywhere you'd like. I don't want to cause you any stress."

"Oh no, it's not that. It's...well...Detective Paul, whom I know you've met and conversed with before, came to see us yesterday."

An itch began at the base of my back and tripped up my spine. "And?"

She leaned forward. "Well, he told us about your gift."

I jerked back slightly and bit my lip to keep from gasping. He told them? How could he?

Her hand to covered my own which currently gripped my napkin. "Please don't be upset. He needed to explain how he obtained some of the information on Debra's case."

I pressed my lips together. "I'd preferred to have told you myself and I thought I had his word he wouldn't reveal that information."

"I'm sorry if that upsets you. But I've always figured you were special."

I lifted my brows. "You did?"

She nodded. "Having lived here all my life, not much happens that I don't get some bits and pieces of conversations when folks come into the store to shop. They never think anyone hears them. I'm glad, actually that it was confirmed so I didn't think I was going crazy."

"Mrs. Haygood...Gladys, it isn't that I didn't trust you."

"Oh, I know that. I am just so grateful you were able to help the detective get answers after all these years."

"Did you know your daughter had passed away?" I blurted out, then bit my lip. Drat.

She blinked. "I had a feeling," she pressed her hand to her chest. "In here. I believed she was gone."

"I am so sorry," I said.

"Thank you. After all this time, I knew if I hadn't heard from her, she was gone. We were too close." She sighed. "Maybe not as close as I thought since she never hinted at running away. I truly believed she agreed that giving her baby up for adoption was for the best. I realize I was wrong about that now. But there is some good which has come from this whole thing."

"There is?" Play stupid.

"Yes. Detective Paul was able to locate our grandson and he agreed to meet with us. In fact, he came by yesterday. He is a very smart young man. He's married now and..." she paused dramatically, before lowering her voice, "I'm going to be a great-grandmother next year. Isn't that divine?"

"Congratulations. That is fantastic news."

"I'm so happy he wants us in his life. He headed home to get his wife and they're coming back to visit this weekend."

"Gladys, I'm so happy for you."

"Thank you. Thank you." She stared at me. "Your turn."

"My turn for what?"

"I did some checking on your gift. You get visions from items, correct?"

I nodded.

"In order to provide information to the detective, you must have had some visions. What item helped you?"

"Oh, yes." I inhaled a deep breath before soldiering on. "I found some...well...many things when I moved into Trinkets, including some personal items set aside by my Aunt Caroline. Since they weren't with the normal inventory, I knew they had been set aside for a reason." I tugged the small bundle out of my pocket and placed it between us on the table. Slowly unwrapping the pins, I continued, "These were among those items."

She gasped, slapping a palm over her mouth staring at the hairpins.

"You recognize them."

She nodded, then tears fell from her eyes as she lifted them. She wrapped her fingers around the set and pressed it against her lips, closing her lids. I waited silently for a moment, then rose and moved around the table to sit beside her. She tugged out a lacy handkerchief from her pocket and held it against her face, crying silently. I placed a hand on her shoulder.

After a few minutes, she sniffed and opened her lids. Very slowly, she opened her fingers to reveal the hairpins and with her other hand touched them reverently. "I'd given these to her hoping they would

give her comfort during her time away from us." She sniffed, blew her nose, then continued. "I even insisted she sell them if she needed more money than what her father intended to give her while she was away. I hated to send her away. But, at the time, we didn't believe we had a choice."

"I understand," I whispered.

She shook her head. "These were given to me by my mother, who received them from her mother." She shifted her gaze toward me. "You got a vision of Debra with these?"

I nodded.

"Could you...would you mind telling me of your visions?"

"Are you sure you want to know?"

She nodded her head vehemently. "Absolutely."

I spent the next hour telling her all the information I'd received from the visions, leaving out the diary entries. No need for her to know Aunt Caroline made notes of her secrets. When I was done, I swallowed down the remaining tea in my cup.

"So very fascinating, this gift of yours. Thank you so much for sharing with me."

"Of course. I'd like to ask you not to tell anyone, though. I'd rather it not become public knowledge."

"Mitch knows, yes?"

"Of course."

"I promise I won't tell anyone. In fact, it'll be just between us. I don't think...no, I know George would not understand."

"How will you explain the hairpins?"

"If you don't mind, I'm going to tell him you found them with some items Bobby gave you to put on consignment. Maybe say a pawn receipt was attached with Debra's name, so you simply returned them to me. It'll ease things between you two and keep your secret."

"I'm good with that. Thank you."

"No, thank you. This means so much to me, I can't explain."

"I'm glad it does." I checked the time. "I'm sorry, but I need to go. We're closing the shop this afternoon to get our allotment of eggs decorated for the hunt.

We hugged and I left. *Okay, so that was not too bad of a reveal.*

Chapter Nineteen

Sunday morning the sun shone bright in the sky with wispy clouds floating allowing a light breeze to break the heat. All the closed shops on Main Street held signs giving directions to the park for Petrie's Crossing Grand Easter Egg Hunt event. Mitch and I held hands as we walked toward the park, nodding at tourists who'd arrived in town and joined the locals. As one group of kids pushed past us, Mitch laughed. I glanced around and spotted Andy's family, along with Nancy making their way toward the park with Bobby and Aurora following behind. I grinned seeing Aurora's father trailing along as well.

"I'm almost sorry I missed this last year," I said watching another group of kids squealing and running to their destination, swinging baskets in their arms.

"Almost?" Mitch asked.

"I don't miss the opportunity to decorate one hundred eggs. I didn't envy Andy and Nancy trying to get the kids to bed Friday night, considering how late it was before they got home. I tried to get him to

leave earlier, but his kids are as stubborn as he is. They all refused to leave until the last egg was done."

"Bless them, or you'd still have been at it until Saturday morning."

"True," I said then grinned. "At least I didn't have to get up at the crack of dawn to hide them. How did you get out of helping with that?"

"Egg boiler only boils the eggs and arranges delivery. That's enough."

We arrived at the park to find Ms. Michelline, her son and his father spreading out several quilts on the grass. She waved us over.

"You've met Vincent when he was in town last month," she said pointing to the handsome man next to her.

"I did. Nice to you see again, Mr. Bossier." We shook hands, then he turned and helped Zach spread out another quilt.

"I brought several for folks to use. This one is for you two," she handed me a pretty brown log cabin patterned quilt.

"Are you sure it's okay to put these on the ground? They're so pretty."

"They're made for using, not displaying and collecting dust."

"Got it. Thanks," I said and handed it to Mitch. "Let's park there," I pointed to a small clearing about three feet away. Waving goodbye, we worked together spreading the quilt on the ground.

"She looks happy," Mitch said lifting his chin toward the group we'd just left.

I glanced back and smiled. "Yeah, maybe Ms. Michelline has decided to give her son's father another chance?"

We sat, then Mitch leaned over and gave me a quick kiss on the cheek. "You're such a romantic."

"I am and I'm not ashamed of it."

I scanned the crowd and gasped when I found Gladys and George entering the park with another younger couple. The woman's pregnancy was very obvious. I discreetly pointed their way, "Look. The Haygood's grandson brought his wife. How sweet is that?"

"Very sweet," Mitch said. "Thanks to you."

I glanced at him. "Not completely."

"Enough," he said sliding his gaze around the crowd of people laughing, chatting and planting their families in spots surrounding the main gazebo where the Mayor sat chatting with his wife. "Do you realize how many people's lives you've changed since moving here?" He asked.

I blinked. "I really haven't thought about it."

"Look there," he said pointing at Marnie and her daughter Chloe, fighting over where to lay their

blanket. "Marnie and her daughter don't have to worry about finances anymore and she's proven to be part of the founders of Petrie's Crossing." He paused, twisted, and then lifted his chin to our right. "Andy's kids are set and he's happy to have settled his land dispute. Nancy's got her precious grandfather's pocket watch."

Bobby escorted Aurora and her father to the edge of the crowd. "Bobby is helping Aurora and she's getting better and better every day. No one pities her anymore."

"Well, okay. I've helped some."

Judy from Rocky's Railroad Museum stood with her hands on her hips and appeared to be arguing with the Mayor. "Judy's still Judy, but now she can boast about her Civil War display, thanks to you."

"I wish she'd mellow some. No matter how much I helped her, she's still not quite nice to me."

"She's been that way for most of her life. No sense holding our collective breath hoping she'll change now."

"True." Clara ran up to us and gave me a hug. "Hello sweetie. You ready to hunt for some eggs?" I asked the eight-year-old.

She nodded causing her curls to bounce around her face. She slid a glance toward Mitch, then leaned down to whisper in my ear. "My friends are going to help me so I can beat my brothers in finding the most eggs this year."

I laughed, shaking my head. "That's cheating, isn't it?"

She frowned, tipped her head to the side, then shook it. "Nope. I know they snuck out earlier this morning to watch the adults hide eggs, so they know some of the spots already. That's cheating."

"You're right. Does your dad know?"

"Yep. He told them they have to share a basket with someone who's younger than me as punishment."

"Aw, that's nice."

The Mayor's voice boomed over the microphone. Clara waved, then ran off back to her father. After the announcements, the Mayor called the kids to the front, making sure everyone had baskets and the younger ones were paired up, he rang a large bell. All the kids screamed and ran off for their hunt.

Mitch leaned close. "What was Clara saying about getting help?"

My face heated. Drat. I'd forgotten to tell Mitch all about Clara's ability to see ghosts. "Later," I said. "Let's enjoy today and I'll tell you all about it, okay?"

"Okay," he responded.

Epilogue

Later that afternoon, Mitch and I sat eating spaghetti and salad on paper plates among the crowded park. The weather granted everyone a beautiful day for the hunt and eating afterwards. Clara had won the competition, of course. Who wouldn't when they had ghosts helping them find the eggs? I finished clearing my plate as Officer Rick walked up carrying a full plate of food.

"Mind if I join you two?" He asked.

"Sure," Mitch said waving toward the unoccupied section of our quilted spot.

Rick sat and waved his fork toward me. "There's like twelve different pies on the tables. If you want your choice, you'd better go hit them now. I saw Bobby heading that way and he said he's going to get himself a slice of each to share with Aurora," he said, then winked.

I jumped up and paused when Mitch burst out laughing. "What?" I asked.

He shook his head. "Nothing. Grab me a slice of apple if there's any left?"

"Okay," I said and rushed off toward the desserts.

"Looks like a great turnout," Steph whispered inside my mind.

I glanced around and dipped my chin.

"I figured it's best to chat inside your head than appear and take a chance anyone else might be able to see me. With this crowd, who knows."

"You're right," I responded. *"Were you one of Clara's helpers?"*

"Heck yeah. That kid is too cute, and it was fun beating everyone."

"You're a bad influence on her if you condone cheating."

"Oh pooh. Anyway, I only wanted to stop by and say hi."

"Thanks." I filled my plate with three slices of different pies, grabbed a second plate and lifted a large piece of apple pie for Mitch.

"You're going to get fat eating so much."

"Bite me." Her laughter echoed in my mind, then faded. I checked out my full plate and shook my head. Nah. I'll burn the calories tonight when I jump Mitch. My body warmed as images of him in bed filled my mind. I stumbled jerking to keep from dropping my plates when a little boy bumped into my legs from behind. I glanced back and froze. His blonde hair caught the sun and glistened with sweat which dripped on the dark blue striped baseball shirt.

My skin chilled suddenly. Little Timmy wore the same colored shirt when he was killed. I swallowed past the bile threatening to push it and my recently downed dinner up my throat. Clenching my jaw, I squeezed my eyes shut shoving the image of Timmy out of my mind. *No. Stop.*

"Oh, I'm so sorry," a young woman said tugging the boy's arm. "Jason. You almost made her drop her food. Apologize right now." She held his shoulders and his sweet baby angel face looked up to me.

"I'm sorry," he whispered.

"It's okay," I croaked out, then sidestepped the boy and his mom and rushed back toward Mitch.

Mitch frowned when he spotted me nearly running at him. He rose and held out his hands, grabbing the plates. "You okay? What happened?"

I shook my head sharply and plopped on my butt, sucking air into my lungs. *Breathe. Breathe.*

"Shannon?" Rick asked. "What's going on?"

My face heated as I glanced between the two. "Nothing really. I bumped into a boy who reminded me of Timmy. I'm fine now." *Please let me be fine.*

Mitch wrapped an arm around my shoulders. "It's okay," he whispered.

"I know," I said forcing my lips to curve into a smile.

Rick opened his mouth to say something, but then closed it staying silent, still watching me.

"I'm fine," I repeated.

He stared then nodded. "I wanted to tell you I had a long talk with Paul."

My neck stiffened. "You mean the guy who can't keep his mouth shut except when it's convenient for him?" I snapped.

Rick winced. "I chewed him out for both of us. He won't do that again, trust me. He won't even put your information in his report."

"Then how's he going to explain where he got her information?" Mitch asked.

"Confidential information, concerned citizen. I told him I didn't care how he phrased it, but I did not want to see Shannon's name anywhere in his report, and I have ways to check to be sure he doesn't."

I nodded, still shaky. "Good."

Rick rose. "I'll let you two be. I only wanted to pass on the information."

Mitch rose and shook his hand. "Thank you."

I waited until he left, before grabbing my dessert plate and shoved a bite of pumpkin pie in my mouth. The sweet sugar sent calm down my body and eased the tightness in my stomach. I sighed.

"You sure you're okay? You want to leave?" Mitch asked.

"No, I don't want to let this ruin the day. I'll be fine. Besides, I love seeing Clara play with other kids," I said pointing toward the swings where she laughed with other girls her age. To distract him, I told him about her gift and caught him up on everything Nancy, Andy, and I had already discussed.

He blinked. "Wow. I never considered one of Andy's kids would turn out like that." He shook his head. "I guess gifts like hers and yours aren't so rare?"

I gave him a small smile. "No. Not so rare. Only in some places, and not discussed openly, I suppose."

He tipped his head toward the little girl playing. "Is she going to be okay?"

"Yeah. Andy seems to have a good grip on her ability. Plus, Nancy brings her by to chat with me. I think it helps her talking to someone who's grown up with a gift like hers." Exactly like hers plus more. I opened my mouth to spill everything about Steph, but stopped. No. I promised Steph and I can't break that promise.

"At least Andy is accepting it, and she has you to help. See? It's not so hard to believe others can accept the fact that mysticism exists after a little adjustment time."

"Adjustment time?"

He leaned in close. "I'm working on it."

"I know," I said. Not everyone is that accepting, but I wasn't going to ruin the day. "You're right."

After finishing our food, we both lay back on the blanket and he held my hand. "Have you chosen your next item yet?" He whispered.

"I think I'm going to do those pearl earrings. They seem to be calling to me."

"How?"

"It's kind of hard to explain. It's like an energy builds, then they seem to shine brighter than the other things," I said. "Does that make sense?"

"For you? Absolute sense."

I turned my head and gazed into his brown eyes with their little gold specks. "Yep. Absolute sense," I said, leaning over and giving him a quick kiss, before dropping back down. Together, we lay there with the sounds of people talking, yelling, and laughing.

Next month I'll have been here a year. One whole year. I stared at the clouds moving along the sky. *A challenging, but good year.* I crossed my fingers on the side away from Mitch. *Please let next year be less challenging, but just as good...or better.*

ABOUT THE AUTHOR

Sherrie Lea Morgan is an active member of Romance Writers of America and her local Chapter Georgia Romance Writers. She lives north of Atlanta, GA with her twin sister, two dogs and two cats. Her goal is to encourage readers to see ghosts in a different way. When not working her current manuscripts, she enjoys spending time with her sister, daughter and son. Although her children refuse to join her paranormal movie thrills, they are supportive in her obsession of all things scary. Of course, they are always willing to travel with her.

www.sherrieleamorgan.com

https://www.facebook.com/sherrielea.morgan

https://mobile.twitter.com/slmorganwrit